Originally I was going to dedicate this book to my children, however in the process of creating the dedication I realized that it was not the case. I love my children dearly but our relationship is strained to say the least. I wanted to believe that by the time *Vengeance Is Mine* was published things would be different. They are not, and my relationship with my children, Zac Bongianino, Heather Brack, Nadia Bongianino, Ben Bongianino and the son I lost to cancer two years ago, Dante Bongianino is as fictional as the stories I write. The fact of the matter is I made terrible mistakes as a father and writing has been my therapy. I apologize to all my children one more time but I do not expect our relationship to ever be repaired. When I write a story I use all the passion, hurt, and rage of all the years that have passed and the distance between my children and I created by my mistakes. May Dante rest in peace and may all my children achieve all of their dreams. Thank you and I hope you enjoy: *Vengeance Is Mine*.

Introduction

I was watching a documentary on serial killers one day and an idea popped in my head. I wondered how many of these killers were still out there? If you are like me then these programs generate questions. I know from other crime shows that serial killers can go on a spree but then suddenly stop, remaining dormant for years. I wondered how many of these cases went unsolved and how many of the killers are still at large. Police and FBI can't solve every case and in many instances it's a question of manpower and politics. The public needs to feel safe and the police have to answer to someone higher up the chain of command. All of this led me to write *Vengeance Is Mine*, a story that explores the possibility of a new avenue to deal with criminals that evade the law. A look at coloring outside the lines of the justice system but in the end getting results. After reading *Vengeance Is Mine* you can decide if justice was served.

Thank You.

Vengeance Is Mine

Where do we go when the laws on which we depend
Are practiced by lawless men
Evil sleeps
In mid-night dreams
Will anyone hear my screams
Violence in my eyes
Blood rains from the sky
Am I dead or alive
Or martyred like Jesus Christ
Holy man speaks in riddles and rhyme
Tells me that vengeance is mine
War is hell
As Satan climbs out from the well
The air smells like death
I can feel it in my sweat
I am a soldier and my mission's clear
Save me from myself, I do not belong here
Too late for me now, I have seen too much
Is this mine, or your blood
Violence lives in my eyes
Bullets rain from the sky
You have forsaken me, Jesus Christ

Now…
And 'till the end of time
Vengeance is mine
Oh, dio, abbi pieta di me

Dave Bongianino

VENGEANCE IS MINE

AUSTIN MACAULEY PUBLISHERS™

LONDON • CAMBRIDGE • NEW YORK • SHARJAH

Ordering Information
Quantity sales: Special discounts are available on quantity purchases by corporations, associations, and others. For details, contact the publisher at the address below.

Publisher's Cataloging-in-Publication data
Bongianino, Dave
Vengeance Is Mine

ISBN 9798889104353 (Paperback)
ISBN 9798889104360 (ePub e-book)

Library of Congress Control Number: 2023914117

www.austinmacauley.com/us

First Published 2024
Austin Macauley Publishers LLC
40 Wall Street, 33rd Floor, Suite 3302
New York, NY 10005
USA

mail-usa@austinmacauley.com
+1 (646) 5125767

20240415

As a young boy, the thought of doing anything other than playing football professionally was absurd. My brother and I watched videos of our dad at Harvard where he played all three linebacker positions. In fact, that is how we were named, William and Samuel. Will is what the coaches call the weakside linebacker, and Sam is the strongside linebacker. If he and Mom had decided to have another, and it was a boy as well, he would have been named Mike for the middle linebacker. As it were, they stopped at two. I often wondered what Dad would have done if we were girls.

My second choice would have to be a Marine. Dad was a Marine, and while he did not talk about his time in the service, Sam and I witnessed the discipline every day of our lives. The way he carried himself and conducted himself, he was a Marine in life, Oorah.

He graduated early from Harvard with a law degree; Dad was wicked smart. He decided that before settling into private practice, he wanted to serve his country. He did a four-year stint in the Marine Corps, honorably discharged with the rank of captain.

A year after he came home, Sam was born. To talk about my brother Sam is to first say that we were two completely different people. I was and am an emotional person, and I do not mind showing that emotion. Probably more like my mom than I like to admit.

Sam, even as an infant, was stone-cold. I can barely remember him crying much, no matter what the situation. Even if he took a bad fall, no tears; it was astonishing. Our dad was a bit like that, but he had no trouble showing how he felt about his children.

Sam was uncomfortable with the affection of any kind. I mentioned our mom; Jenna Mancini was her maiden name. A full-blooded Italian girl complete with all the passion and temper as well. She was five-foot-six, and Dad was six-foot-two; we called them mini and mighty. Dad was German/Irish and, as I mentioned, wicked smart.

He often told us the smartest thing he ever did was marry our mom. We agreed. Sam inherited Mom's temper and Dad's muscular physique. I got Dad's intelligence and Mom's looks. As Sam grew older, I could tell he was a tough kid, a fighter, not a bully, on the contrary. He seemed to protect the weak, those that could not protect themselves.

Dad and I started calling him Cujo because he was thick and had a ferocious temper. When he got angry, he was like a rabid dog. Despite the age difference, five years between us, he still followed me around. I did not mind; he was a good kid.

I could get away with picking on him, to a point. Once when he was like ten years old, we were wrestling in the living room. I had him pinned, but I decided to show off a little first. I looked into his eyes to let him know that I was the big brother, but he was not moving or resisting, and his eyes were closed, the lids fluttering. I let up on him, and then he opened his eyes and smiled at me, flipping me over onto my back for the pin.

He told me he was just letting me know that he could win at any time. He was ten; I was fifteen. I will never forget that moment. I was the smart one, so I let my brother have that one; I was the handsome one too.

We always laughed about that; I was the perfect likeness to my dad when he was my age. So my mom liked to tell me anyway. Sam did not look like Mom or Dad, but he was Mom's favorite. Mom was the only person that could calm him down when he went all Cujo.

I breezed through high school, and of course, college was in my future. Harvard, like Dad and Mom, both legacies. That is where Dad met our mom; she had a business degree. As I said, I inherited my dad's intelligence, but Mom was smart too. I had an insatiable appetite for life and the answers to questions, all questions.

I must have been annoying to both my parents, but they humored me. Sam struggled with school, not because he was slow or stupid. He just had a problem coloring within the lines. It was authority, but there were never disciplinary issues. He just did better going it alone.

Figuring things out using his instincts more than reading the instructions. Mom and Dad stood by him as he found his own way in his young life, and so did I. We both played high school football; I was the quarterback of the varsity team. Sam played linebacker like Dad only in junior varsity. He came to see me play, and I was always there to watch him.

Once I threw a late interception in a close game and when I tried to make the tackle, I got hit from behind and hurt my shoulder. Our defense held, and we won, but I remember Sam caught up to the guy who hit me after the game. It took Mom and Dad both to keep him from hurting a boy that was three years older and fifty pounds heavier. I have never seen anyone hit so hard or fast as my brother, on or off the field.

Every Saturday morning, we played pickup football with Dad and the neighbor's kids, then ordered pizza, and watched college football. If Harvard was on, it was like a national holiday. Family and friends came over; Mom cooked a feast; and we made a day of it.

As I mentioned before, Sam was a different boy around our mom. He was dialed in, and there was something in his eyes. He loved that woman, and it showed. Still not the emotional type, that was me and Dad, but caring and attentive. Sam was a loner; he kept to himself much of the time.

Even in a crowded room filled with friends or family, he drifted off by himself. Never a problem for the family, but others viewed him as difficult. You go along to get along, I guess. He had a fascination for knives; one Christmas, Dad got him a pocketknife. Sam loved that knife and carried it on him everywhere, all the time.

Mom was a bit of an outdoors person as a young girl; she had a collection of throwing knives that she pulled out from time to time and showed off. Sam, of course, started throwing his pocketknife but with no success. Mom broke down and gave him her throwing knives and showed him how to throw. I never understood the appeal, but Mom and Sam spent hours throwing and talking. My dad, Thomas

Edward Calloway, was my hero, and Jenna Isabel Mancini Calloway, our mom, was Sam's hero.

As I mentioned, Saturdays were all about football, but Sunday was Mom's day. Mom was born and raised as a Catholic in a strict religious family. It was a challenging thing for Sam and me to wrap our brains around, but one day, Dad put it all in perspective for us. He was not a religious man, but he saw the passion that Mom had and went along. Mom believed that faith was about discipline, and Dad was down with discipline.

Mom always told us that believing in a higher power, something better than us, kept us humble. It did. Sometimes, at night before bed, she would read from the Bible. It varied depending on circumstances, but she believed there was a message, an important message in the scripture. At times, she embellished or paraphrased or, as Dad liked to say, put it in her own words.

One such verse stuck with us; it was: 'Behold I send an Angel before you, to protect and secure you. Fear not if you are just and kind, but if you are of an evil mind, then vengeance will be mine'. She would always finish with something in Latin: Oh dio, Abbi, pieta di me. We came to realize that meant; Oh, lord, have mercy on me. That was our mom.

As high school graduation neared for me, I could not help but think about college life. Harvard law school was one of the tops in the country, and I was on a football scholarship. Could life get any better? I was eighteen; Sam just turned thirteen, and all he could talk about was joining the Marines.

Always mature for his age and absolutely having no interest in college, he wanted to enlist right now. However, we made a pact to enlist together, so he would have to wait to graduate high school, and by then, I would be done with law school.

On one terrible, horrible night, our lives would change forever. Dad and I went to the movies; Mom and Sam went for pizza. Dad's phone went off about halfway through; he grabbed me by the arm and told me we had to go. He did not speak in the car, but I could tell something was very wrong. I could not take the silence anymore, just as we arrived at the scene. He told me to wait in the car; I told him there was no fuckin' chance.

The ambulance was already there, parked beside Mom's car. It was all but demolished; they were putting the neck brace on her; she was not conscious. Sam was at her side and did not even acknowledge Dad or me. We tried to get him to let go, and Dad would stay with Mom, but he lashed out in a violent rage. The look in his eyes frightened us both.

The paramedics loaded her into the ambulance, and my little brother went with our mom to the hospital. Dad and I followed; still, he did not speak to me. We pulled into St. John, the Baptist hospital.

As they took our mom to the emergency room, Sam had to let go now. That is when I noticed he was bleeding from his head. I told Dad about the cut, and he went to talk to Sam. Sam was not in a talking mood, and we all knew it was best to leave him as he sat quietly, alone staring at the wall. He was mumbling something, but from where we were, we could not make it out.

It seemed like hours when the doctor came into the room, and his body language suggested unwelcome news. The exact order of events after that is still unclear, but our mom had passed away from blunt force trauma to her head. Dad began to cry, and I went to him. He was a big man, but I had to hold him up or he would collapse. I reached for Sam, but he was gone. I had to leave my dad alone, concerned for the well-being of my little brother.

He would not stop despite my pleas. When I finally caught up to him, I asked where he was going. He told me that he was going to kill that motherfucker.

I asked him, "Who?"

He told me, "Who did I think? The driver."

I looked at him; the blood now dried on his head from hours ago; and I told him that Mom was gone and that would not bring her back. Then my fourteen-year-old brother broke down and cried like I had never seen him before. He got weak in his knees as our dad came to us and held us both. As we stood, there the ambulance brought in another injured person, a woman. We believed it was the driver that hit Mom and Sam.

The paramedics asked us to move, and we could tell by their faces it was the person responsible for our mom's death. Dad held us tight, but Sam wiggled free and approached the woman on the stretcher. The medics asked him again to move away, but he ignored them and walked right up to her; she was in a bad way.

Dad let me go and called out to Sam. He just stood there and looked into her eyes. Dad grabbed him by the arm, but all Sam did was make a sign of the cross on her forehead and say these words: Oh Dio, Abbi, pieta di me. The woman did not live.

Time can be subjective, depending on your perspective. College life had been good for me; I had an IQ of 179, so I breezed through my courses like I did in high school. Playing quarterback for the Harvard Crimson was as rewarding as graduating early, Summa Cum Laude. I can see now why Mom and Dad both came here.

Met a girl, Emily, but nothing serious.

My thoughts were turning now to going back to Warm Springs Virginia and fulfilling the promise I made to my brother, enlisting in the Marines together. Mom passed away four years ago; Dad took some time off from practicing law. He drove up to see me often, and when he was not here, I would drive to Warm Springs to see him and my brother.

Sam had grown and filled out; he was muscular like Dad. He changed since Mom was gone; he was always a loner, but now he hardly spoke. He spent hours practicing with his knives; he had gotten proficient at throwing. When we got together, I did most of the talking. He had a way with the truly little conversation of getting to the heart of things. He was about to turn eighteen and, in many ways, more of a man than most his age. I got his attention when the subject of enlisting came up.

Dad and he were close now, and he worried about Dad's health. He told me Dad was not taking care of himself like before. I assured him that Dad was as tough as ever, and he should be excited about doing the one thing we dreamed about as kids. Being a soldier. I changed the subject to my girlfriend, Emily; we had been dating off and on since my freshman year.

Sam asked why off and on. I told him that she was not a supporter of me enlisting. I made myself clear at the beginning, but women like to think they can change man's mind. Sam asked why enlisting was a problem. I told him that her father served but never made it home.

Sam told me she would come around and he was anxious to meet her. Emily James was someone I could see myself settling down with after my four-year term is up. I must admit I saw some of Mom in Emily. She would arrive later that day as Sam and I would announce to family and friends that we were going to be Marines.

Family and friends gathered in the living room as if they did not already know what I was about to announce. My dad stood proudly beside his two boys, and everyone was pleased, except Emily. She took me by the arm into the next room. She was not pleased. She told me she expected me to talk more about the decision with her before committing.

I told her my intentions were clear and I was sorry if she felt ambushed, but it was a dream of my brother and mine to enlist together. She was trembling and in tears as she expressed concern for my safety. I told her that this was the proudest moment of my life, and I wanted her support. She told me she loved me for the first time and would pray for me every day and left the room.

Sam noticed the emotional state Emily was in and offered a solid piece of advice. He told me that God only made one Jenna Calloway, give this girl a break. Agreed.

I must admit I had reservations about Sam in the Marines, especially after Mom passed. He was even more withdrawn, even more monotone, even more willful, and prone to reject authority. Mom was the calm to his storm. However, he adjusted quite well to a soldier's life. He was obedient and hard-working.

Camp Lejeune in Jacksonville, North Carolina, was a little over a six-hour drive from Warm Springs, Virginia. Dad visited often and brought letters from Emily, friends, and family. On one occasion, he brought gifts. For Sam, a nine-inch, bone-handled straight knife with a leather sheath and one of his throwing knives for good luck. For me, he brought a pocket journal; he felt that I could document the life of a Marine. Something he would love to read when we got back, and something he could not trust Sam to do.

Sam tucked the throwing knife in his boot, and the bone-handled knife went on his belt, for good. I put the journal in my pocket and promised to record as much as possible. We were in the thirteenth week of basics and soon would be sent to Camp Lemonier in Africa. There, we could be deployed for up to a year before a trip home.

Dad knew that this would be the last time he would see us for a while. Tom Calloway was a big man, six foot two, two hundred thirty pounds, and a Marine, but on this day, he showed us his softer side. He held back a tear as he told us how proud he was to be our father and would not have peace until we were back home. He stood tall and saluted us both and told us our mother would be proud as well. Sam never flinched; I cried like a baby.

I now know why they say Africa is hot because it is a different hot. In full pack, a man had to be in top shape to survive the heat. Adjusting to it and just the idea of being so far from home was harder on me than I expected. Sam had no problem adjusting; he seemed at home in the worst conditions. They say war is hell, and now I know why.

We continued basics, but it was more about getting ready to be a unit. Alpha 1 was our unit, made up of seven guys from all over the USA. Ben Wilson, from Pennsylvania, was our leader, with the rank of captain. He was on his second tour, another four-year term. The others were Greg, Josh, Barry, and Kevin.

Captain Wilson, myself, and Sam were in Alpha 1. Sam was the youngest of us all at the ripe youthful age of nineteen. But, as he has proven his whole life so far, the boy had guts and was tough as a $2 steak.

When Marines are bored, they do crazy shit. Some passed the pigskin around; some like Sam picked fights. Not one to shy away from a fistfight with anyone; he knew these guys were some of the toughest in the world.

So, obviously, my little brother wanted to see just how tough it was. They would make a circle, wrap up their hands with socks and tape, and square off. It was all wholesome fun, that is, if you are a Marine. To everyone's surprise, except mine, Sam beat everyone in camp. As I said before, I have never seen anyone hit so fast and hard. It was his gift.

Our unit would be sent to Afghanistan where thirty-two of thirty-four provinces are Taliban controlled. We set up for maneuvers in the province of Kabul.

When approaching any hostile territory, we aired on the side of caution. Our point man was originally supposed to be Barry, but he won a coin flip and put Sam out front. Sam relished the opportunity. Captain Wilson told me that Sam had a little Rambo in him. I told Ben we used to call him Cujo back home, but he has not gone by that name in years.

Our intelligence was that hostiles were making a move on Kabul, meaning they would invade and put it under Taliban rule. Our mission was reconnaissance, observing and reporting. However, we were given the go-ahead to engage the enemy if fired upon. We all hoped it did not come to that.

Captain Wilson and I got to know each other on a personal basis with this mission. He had stories to tell, and I listened. He told me on his last tour of duty he and his unit were in Nepal, a village in Southeast Asia. His unit was on a rescue mission; hostiles had taken prisoners. They went into the mountainous terrain on a rainy night.

Using night vision, they located the rebel base and set up a perimeter. They were about to engage with some cover fire and smoke grenades when a hostile dragged a body outside; a naked woman. He had her head in one hand as he dragged her with the other. I gave the command to take the camp. All we heard was screaming and a hailstorm of gunfire.

It only lasted for a few minutes, but the memory of that night still haunts me. I asked about the prisoners. Ben told me they were all dead, what one human being can do to another. That is true horror. It is funny how silence can speak sometimes; I felt an eerie sense that something was wrong.

Entering the narrow pass that led to the village, we were single file; Sam was out of my view. I scanned the area, and something caught my eye. I do not even know what it was, but my gut told me to get down. Suddenly, it was raining bullets on us; rooftop snipers had us in a cross fire.

Ben gave the order to hold position and go back-to-back and return fire. Barry was hit; he went down; I dragged him back, but he was in a bad way. This did not look good, pinned down in a cross fire. As I began to recite a prayer, it seemed as if the snipers were either reloading or taking a better position. Maybe a dream but the silence was speaking to me again.

I heard our captain yell to someone to get down; it was Sam. He came back to us, gun blazing; he laid down enough cover fire for us to get out of that heat. Sam told Ben that there were two snipers; now there was one. He did not see any other hostiles in the area.

Ben told him that was excellent work but to try not to go all Rambo again. It was at that time we realized that Barry was gone. Barry Jones from Minnesota, a good Marine and trusted friend. This was the first time I witnessed death. I choked back a tear and recited a verse I remembered from my youth: 'I will be an enemy of your enemy, an adversary to your adversaries, and I will make them bleed'.

'Oh Dio, Abbi, Pieta Di Me.'

A Marine Detachment or MarDet was a unit of thirty-five to eighty-five US Marines. Aboard this aircraft carrier, we reported to our captain, R.J. Melnick. We debriefed, got medical attention, and then ate. Before sleep, Captain Melnick requested Alpha 1 leader, Ben Wilson, and I to report to his quarters.

Captain Melnick was old school, career Marine, and a man of few words. He commended us on the effort and offered condolences on the loss of a team member. He then turned his attention to my brother Sam. He asked if we had a problem, and if it should be addressed. I looked at Ben to gauge his reaction, but he spoke up and assured the captain that there was not a problem.

In other words, he trusted Sam, and that meant a lot to me. Captain Melnick finished by saying no more Rambo shit though. We both agreed. From the aircraft carrier to Camp Lemonier, Djibouti, a small village on the coast of Africa, we got to unwind before the next mission. We had been deployed for a little over six months.

A chance to feel human again, some of the guys liked to read the juicy details of letters from girlfriends back home. It was a nice release and mostly lies anyway. When the sergeant major called out our names, Samuel and William Calloway, I got anxious. It would be the first time I heard from Emily and Dad in a while. I was not as public as the others, but that did not stop them from prying.

Sam went off by himself as he always does. I decided to humor the boys with the first line from Emily's letter. It read: 'I am sorry to have to tell you this in a letter but…'. I stopped reading aloud and looked around the room to see that no one wanted to hear what came next. They went about their business as I snuck out of the room.

The letter went on to say that Emily had deep feelings for me, but since I was gone, she met someone. She did not mean for it to happen, but my decision to become a Marine forced her to realize she was not cut out for this life. My first thought was how could I be so wrong about someone. Someone that reminded me of our mom in so many ways. Mom had fears too; she told us about them, but she embraced the fact that the man she loved wanted to serve his country.

Sam had heard about the Dear John letter and came to see how I was doing. I told him I felt foolish; I felt like I missed a sign or something. Sam told me that Emily had good qualities, not the least of which was picking me as a boyfriend. He told me having feelings for someone was not foolish, but he reminded me again that God only made one Jenna Mancini Calloway, and I should stop measuring women by her; it was too high of a mountain for others to climb.

He then told me something that stuck. He told me he could see me settling down with a good woman, a brilliant woman, and said, "Because brother you are the smartest person I have ever met."

He went on to say that I would have a couple of brilliant kids. He told me my kids would cure cancer, become president, stop world hunger, and do amazing things with their lives. He told me he expected remarkable things from me because I was that fuckin' brilliant. He smiled at me, and of course, I teared up. Sam did not talk much, but when he did, it counted.

Our next mission was meeting up with the Alpha 2 unit in Tajikistan; they had been on recon just outside the village. Their intel had a rebel force setting up nearby in the mountainous area. A hostile environment. Tajikistan is a poor country dominated by mineral extractions and metal processing. The US Embassy warns citizens to reconsider traveling in the area.

We would fly out of Djibouti into a base camp about 100 kilometers (about 62.14 mi) from Tajikistan. About 4,600 kilometers (about 2,858.31 mi). We were briefed on the mission, and our captain, Ben Wilson, got us together to make the message clear: "This is hostile territory; Alpha 2 has not checked in at the scheduled time. We are to assume they have engaged or are still engaged with the enemy. We will proceed to their rendezvous spot and conduct a sweep of the area."

He finished by telling us it was rough terrain, and it looked like rain, a piece of cake. Rain was an understatement, a downpour that made the hike much more difficult. Sam was up ahead of us as usual, just out of view. Ben and I were in the middle as Josh, Kevin, and Greg fell in behind us.

This was a real-life nightmare, but it gave Ben time to reminisce about past missions. He told me it was common for people in these villages to strap bombs to dogs and send them into the streets. It was common to have rebels to use women and children as shields in a gunfight. Women gang raped in a public square, and men too.

Families were forced to watch loved ones tortured and killed in a brutal fashion. You cannot unsee these things. I had not been writing in my journal as much lately. I lost interest after Emily's letter. But I am going to start again soon. We heard shots up ahead and double-timed it to see.

I was first on the scene. Sam was in a standoff with a rebel. I could not get a clear shot and did not know why Sam was just standing there. He dropped his weapon, reached for his knife, and sent it flying at the hostile. The knife planted firmly in the forehead of its intended target. The rebel slumped over and went down.

As I got closer to the scene, I saw three dead rebels, all clean headshots. I saw a woman with her throat slashed, and Sam was now pulling his knife from the rebel's head. He cleaned it and returned it to its sheath. Ben and the others came in behind me, admiring my brother's work. Ben picked up Sam's gun and looked at the magazine, three shots, three dead rebels.

I am not even going to ask about the knife; that's just more Rambo shit. He shook his head, and we searched the camp but found no one else. Dead or alive, as we surveyed the situation, Ben got word that we were to abort the mission and return to the rendezvous spot. I looked at Ben and asked if he thought that was the right thing to do. He told me that was the order.

I told him something did not feel right; we are leaving soldiers behind. He told me that despite my brother acting like Rambo, this was not a movie. The good guys do not always get the bad guys, and we are not all heroes. Sometimes, we just follow orders. I told him I had a gut feeling that Alpha 2 was here and not far.

He looked at me and told me Alpha 2 was eliminated. I could not accept that; we were too close; their families deserved to know. Ben took a deep breath and agreed. Sam was already on the move, and Ben gave the order for the unit to move. We were single file and proceeding down a narrow-wooded pass for about a mile.

If we did not find anything, we would double back and proceed to the pickup spot. Ben and I had gotten close during this time; Sam was always off by himself. Ben felt like the older brother I never had. He began to tell me about his wife and three children back in Pennsylvania. He told me on his next leave he was finally taking her on the honeymoon he promised her three children ago.

He said they were going to Hawaii; they talked about it for a long time and had saved enough money to go. He told me that he was not lucky enough to be stationed in Hawaii, but the time was right. I asked about the kids; he told me they were coming too. He then told me something that hit home; he said being a wife of a soldier is a hard life. It takes a special woman to deal with the absence and the fact that we are not the same people coming out that they knew going in.

I told him I could relate that my dad was a Marine and… well my ex-girlfriend could not deal. Before I could explain, Sam came out of the brush and put his finger to his mouth to tell us to be quiet. He led us down the path to an opening where six men hung from a tree. They were burned beyond recognition. Dog tags lay on the ground beneath each one.

It was the Alpha 2 unit. We stood in disbelief for a minute; then Sam went back into the brush. Ben picked up a dog tag to make sure it was one of ours. Greg, Kevin, and Josh formed a circle around us as we surveyed the area; then shots were fired. We did not have time to react, and Ben was hit; he fell in front of me.

As I reached for him, I caught a glimpse of light and returned fire. We all fell to the ground as the shots were coming from all directions. Greg was hit; we returned fire in all directions; and I ordered the men to aim low to the ground. Just as all seemed lost, I heard someone yell, "incoming." A grenade went off right behind us, and I ordered the men again to fire in the same direction I was firing.

The smoke cleared; the sound of gunfire stopped ringing in my ears. I looked up to see Sam standing there asking if everyone was all right. My mind could not process all that had just happened. My ears were buzzing, but I was alive. I reached down and turned Ben over; he was dead.

Greg was hurt but alive; Josh and Kevin were shaken but good. I asked Sam what happened. He told me the rebels had dug pits about fifty yards from this spot. They knew we would come here and find the bodies. They knew we would be sitting ducks and just waited.

I asked about the grenade. He told me that it was him; that we were in his line of fire, so he lobbed one over our heads hoping to take out a few of the hostiles. He told me that we did the rest and asked how I knew to shoot low. I told him I did not have a clue. Just lucky, I guess.

Sam looked at me knowing I was feeling Ben's death. I told him that bullet could have easily been mine. Sam made a sign of the cross and said, "Oh, dio, Abbi, Pieta, Di Me."

Having been deployed for a full year, it was time for leave, but not before debriefing. Captain Melnick requested a conversation with me and Sam. He began by offering condolences for our loss. I felt obligated to tell the whole story at this point. I began by telling the captain that I disobeyed orders.

He asked me how so. I told him Ben had received orders to abort and return, but I felt strongly that we should keep looking for Alpha 2. I convinced him to continue the search; it was my fault. The captain interrupted and reminded me that Ben was in charge; therefore, it was his decision to continue, not yours, Marine. He reminded me that we found Alpha 2, and now their bodies will be retrieved, and they will be given a proper Marine burial.

He reminded me that there were dead hostiles in that mountain as well. He told me he failed to see my point. I told him Ben would be alive if I had just kept my mouth shut. Then the captain spoke on a personal level. He told me and Sam that Ben was a Marine and this was war.

I said, "I know, war is hell."

He told me that was bullshit. War is worse than hell. He asked me who went to hell. I told him sinners; I believe.

He said, "That is right if you are in hell, you deserve to be there; no one innocent goes to hell. In war, there are innocent people that die needlessly. Women and children are slaughtered. You have seen this; you have seen the brutality. Hell is a step up from where you two have been.

"Ben Wilson was a Marine, a damn good Marine. He died serving his country, and you had nothing to do with his death. You are pissed off, I get that, but war killed Ben Wilson, not you. Having said that, I am recommending both you and Sam for field promotions. William Calloway will now have the rank of first lieutenant, and Samuel Calloway will have the rank of second lieutenant."

Sam and I looked at each other and seemed to both have the same thought.

Sam spoke this time; he said that was fine but what we really wanted was purple hearts for Barry Jones and Ben Wilson. The captain asked if we were doing his job now. I told him that the families of both needed to know what kind of Marines and men they were. Captain Melnick said that was already done. He told us he knew of our father; he had never met him, but he heard things.

He asked us if we knew anything about his time in service. We both said no; he did not talk about it much.

Captain Melnick told us he was a Raider, Special OPs. A smart SOB. Sam and I knew nothing of this; Dad was very private about his time in the Marines.

Captain Melnick told us, "Soldiers do not talk about their tour because they do not know how. How do you tell someone that has not been here what you two witnessed? This is not a casual conversation you can have with just anyone. Most soldiers want to forget, but they cannot; this shit becomes a part of you. You do not just flip a switch when you are back in Topeka, Kansas."

I told him it was Warm Springs, Virginia.

He told us, "Whatever… my point is your father wears this but does so privately. Some soldiers never adjust, but you two will just like your father did. Now go home, eat a cheeseburger, get laid, whatever. He stood, saluted us, and said we were dismissed."

The plane ride from Camp Djibouti to Camp Lejeune was long and quiet. My thoughts were random, everything from the past year on a loop in my mind. Sam sat beside me sleeping like a baby. If I closed my eyes, I saw Ben's face. Then Barry's, then gunfire, then grenade shrapnel, dead bodies hanging from trees.

I wondered when or if I could erase these images. I turned my attention to getting back to Warm Springs and seeing my dad. I had many questions for him now, and I hoped he might let me into his secret life as a Marine Raider. Sam woke up and asked if we were there yet. I asked him if he was anxious to be home. He told me he missed Dad and pizza.

He said he was ordering a Big Joe 24 cut with pepperoni and mushrooms. Sam was approaching his twentieth birthday, and I could not help but be proud of how my little brother had grown up. He still was a quiet person, but his actions spoke volumes about his character. I wanted to tell him these things, but I knew I would tear up and Sam hated emotional situations. I told him instead that I was thinking about my future.

I always believed that after serving, I would just go into practicing law. Now, I had second thoughts. I told him that after the things we had witnessed, I wanted to make a difference in the world. He stopped me and told me no matter what I chose to do I would be great at it. He told me he admired the soldier I became, and he knew I was destined for remarkable things.

I thought to myself, 'This is exactly what I was going to say to him'.

He told me I would make a difference because I always do. He told me I would be best at being a father and husband. That was my true destiny. He looked at me, and I began to tear up.

I noticed he was not wearing his dog tags. I asked him about it, and he told me he never wore them around his neck; they bothered him. He kept them in his pocket but lost them in the jungle somewhere. That was typical Sam right there.

He got serious for a moment and talked about the men we lost. He talked about the Notification Officer's job and how to tell someone that the person they were waiting for is not coming home, and he would not want that job. That was not typical Sam.

Dad met us at Camp Lejeune; he looked good and lost a little weight but still a welcome sight. There was so much to say, and I suddenly realized that I did not want to talk about my experiences, not even to the one person that would understand. I wanted to be William or Will again, not private Calloway. Excuse me, that would be First Lieutenant Calloway.

I wanted to see people I had not seen in a year. I wanted to sleep in my bed. I wanted to watch football. I wanted to feel normal again. Sam just wanted to get pizza. Warm Springs, Virginia, was a six-and-a-half-hour drive from Camp Lejeune. I enjoyed every mile of that drive like a kid on his way to Disneyland.

Dad asked Sam if he wanted to stop for pizza, but he wanted Big Joe's. Big Joe was a bar/restaurant where Mom and Dad got pizza every weekend. It was our favorite. I had to admit I was looking forward to a slice as well. Dad did not change a thing about the house.

Everything was just as it was when we left a year ago. Everything. Sam went to his room and closed the door like he always did. Dad told me some things would never change; he was going to pick up the pizza, and I decided to ride along. I wanted to ask about his time in the Marines and specifically about the Raiders, but I did not know how.

Dad was a private man when it came to this subject. In fact, there was nothing in the house to suggest he ever served. We engaged in small talk, but he knew there was something on my mind. When we got back home, Sam was outside throwing knives. He and Mom made a target together after Dad told them they were going to kill the old oak tree in the backyard.

The target, like everything else, was still in the same spot. Sam was skilled at throwing, and it was one of the few times he liked to talk. He asked me if we could choose where we were stationed. I told him that was doubtful. He said that being stationed in Hawaii would be like a vacation. I agreed.

He said, Okinawa would be cool too, but I know we will be back in Djibouti for the next three years. I agreed again. He then asked me if I talked to Dad… about… you know, the Raiders?

I told him, "No; I did not know how."

He said, "OK, I will."

And he called for him to come outside.

In the meantime, he showed me how he kept his lucky throwing knife in his boot for a year and how it left a mark on his leg. He said he was going to make a boot sheath. I was about to ask why when Dad came into the room. Sam just blurted it out, with no hesitation.

He asked our dad why he never told us about the Raiders. My dad looked at us both and said he was tired and going to bed. He told us we were going to see some of his old friends tomorrow and then left the room.

We were all early risers, and the coffee smelled so good. Dad and I were two cup guys; Sam hated coffee and opted for a big glass of orange juice. Eggs, bacon, and hash browns just like Mom made every Sunday morning. It was good to be home. Dad asked me if I was still considering practicing law. I was surprised at the question because I never told him any different.

I told him, "I thought we could be partners and laughed."

He told me he would like nothing more, but he knew me too well. I told him I had an epiphany in the mountains of

Tajikistan. He just sat there listening intently, sipping coffee. I want to make a difference, not that law is not important, but I do not think I can sit at a desk until later in life, much later.

Dad got up from the table and asked Sam if he was coming. Most of the time, Sam would just stay home by himself, but this time, he said he was coming. He told me to take my time finishing breakfast and went outside to be with Sam. I should have realized where we were going and why: the American Legion, one of at least one-hundred Veteran Services Organizations.

Dad was a member, but this was the first time he brought us. When we walked into the room, it was like Dad became a different person. The age groups were as diversified as the personalities. It was like a fraternity, the energy, and comradery. Dad made his way around the room shaking hands and cracking jokes.

I thought this is not the Thomas Calloway I know. A man in a wheelchair presented himself to me and asked if I was the chief's son. I asked who the chief was, and he just laughed. Sam decided to go off by himself and find others to talk to, not like him at all. For the first time in my life, I was the one out of place.

There were a couple of guys sitting at a table waving at me to come over. There was a man in his sixties with a prosthetic arm, a woman in her mid-forties, and another guy that could have been in his nineties. They asked to sit, and I did. The man in his sixties did most of the talking, asking about my time over there. I was not sure how to handle this, not knowing these people, but obviously, they were vets, so I told them it was life-changing, brutally life-changing.

They all agreed. I was stumbling over my words now when the woman took over the conversation. She told me it was OK to be alive and whole. Do not let the guilt eat you up. We all know what we are getting into when we sign up. Not all of us come back, and sometimes, we leave pieces of ourselves over there.

She showed me her leg, or where it used to be. I wanted to get deeper, but she stopped me again, telling me war is not for thinking; it is for surviving. The only life lesson worth learning and holding onto is making it home. You see things and want to know why because they make no sense. It is war; there is no sense.

You come home, and people treat you differently. They thank you for your service, then walk away only glad they did not have to do anymore. They will help provided they do not have to look at us or get to know us. They are just thankful they did not have to do what we did. They call us heroes; we are not.

She looked at me and asked me if I felt like a hero. I told her no, I do not. She said we are soldiers, that's all. There are no heroes, just survivors. They give us parades and our own special day, but all that does for me is keep reminding me of something I want to forget. As I sat there listening, it started to sink in why Dad never talked about it.

No one does; they want to lead normal lives. It is so hard to erase the memories, especially if you are constantly reminded. Even when they got together, they talked about everything but serving. They did not have to; they wore it like the very clothes they wear. Dad and Sam came to get me, and I excused myself.

I asked Dad about the name chief; he just laughed. We spent hours there talking and laughing; it felt like family. The ride home was quiet.

That night while Sam and I watched a little cable television, Dad came in and asked for a minute. I shut off the TV. He told us that when he got back from his tour, he told our mom everything. She wanted to know. When he was done, she made him promise never to tell us boys.

He said, "Now that you have been there, you should know why. There are no mementos in this house because this is our home, yours, and mine. I am not a Marine here, and neither are you. This is your mom's home, and that is how she wanted it. I have my ghosts and demons just like you, but I bury them deep and fight quietly every day to keep them buried. Some soldiers never leave the war; some come home and bring it with them; some lose the fight to keep their demons buried; and some just keep fighting."

I spoke up and told my dad my decision got a man killed. He told me no son; war killed him. He told us he loved us and went to bed. Sam looked at me and told me that was the second person who said that to me, so let it go.

The next morning, Dad and I woke way before Sam. He made coffee, and I sat at the table reading the journal that he gave me. He sat down with his coffee and told me that I would have all the answers if life were a book or a subject in school. The answers are clear when the questions are in test form.

But life is not like that, and my appetite for solutions is the thing that will drive me to bigger things. He told me never to stop looking for the answers even if there appear to be none.

I told him I was worried about Sam. He asked why. I told him he had a death wish.

He told me, "No son, your brother is so much like your mom. That is why they were so close. Neither of them showed their fears, they believed it was a sign of weakness. Your brother watched your mom die; he held her hand and knew she was gone way before the doctor proclaimed it. He had to process that as a child, something someone so young should never have to process.

"He came out the other side, changed forever, but now he has no fear. He does not have a death wish. You and I are scared, afraid for those we love, afraid of the unknown, and, most of all, afraid of failure. Sam just lives without those fears. He just lives."

I told him I missed our mom and then could not help but break down; he held me and told me that our mom gave him the two best sons a father could ever have.

Sam finally woke up and came into the kitchen, looking at us wondering what was happening. He asked what we were talking about. I told him we were talking about his Rambo shit. He grabbed a half gallon of milk and went outside to throw. I gave my journal to my dad and told him to read it after we left. I told him I do not think I need to write anymore.

He took it and said he would read it and then put it with his stuff locked away in storage. Three months in Warm Springs flew by, and it was time to head back to Camp Lejeune. Sam and I said our goodbyes and gave our dad permission to start dating. He told us he enjoyed his life, and it was not time yet.

We called it; we were sent back to Camp Djibouti; and General Anderson wanted a word. He introduced me to Captain Trey Johnson, our new unit leader. He addressed me as First Lieutenant William Calloway. It was a pleasure to meet Trey. I had heard good things about him. General Anderson then informed us we would be transferred to Camp Gonsalves in Okinawa.

He went on to explain the strategic importance of the base camp. He told us there were eighteen thousand Marines stationed in the Indo-Pacific. Okinawa is one of the Ryukyu chains of islands. It is the strategic crossroads for the III Marine Expeditionary Force and that allowed for ease of deployment to the surrounding area. The purpose of military involvement in this area is to improve JMSDF tactical capabilities, to strengthen cooperation, and for peace and stability.

He told us we would be flown to the US Ronald Regan and there meet with Commander Willis. He would brief us on everything from Ukraine War to the Chinese resurgents that insist they do not exist. He finished by telling us we would be teaming up with a new Alpha unit. I met up with Sam who was trying to set up a bare-knuckle tournament but had few takers. I told him about the plans and just asked when we would leave. I told him now.

Aboard the US Ronald Regan, we met with Commander Willis. He briefed us on the work we would be doing. We would spend the next three years of our tour in Okinawa. The culture and atmosphere in Okinawa are a blend of Chinese and Japanese, known as the Hawaii of Japan; it was a remarkable sight.

Too bad we had to go to work. If there were a Chinese resurgent, it would start in a village called Elephant Trunk Hill. We had intel that a base camp was in the making there. Our job, for now, is to work with our new team and integrate the new parts. Captain Trey is a couple of years older than me, reminding me a little of Ben Wilson. We exchanged stories of missions and men we knew, lost, and remembered.

He seemed like a down-to-earth guy. Until he met Sam. You either loved Sam for who he was and the results of his actions or hated him because he went outside the lines consistently. Trey was not a fan of the things he heard. Trying to pull Sam in was like trying to hold back the ocean with a rake.

He was not defiant or disrespectful, just independent; he worked so well alone; and our last unit saw positive results. But this was a new unit and a new leader; he might have to adjust. We would fly in from the US Ronald Regan to the coast of China, a seven-hour flight. Now our intel had the resurgent base camp set up in Fujan, which was much closer to Wenzhou, where we landed. Just three and a half hours away.

The Chinese will swear they have no interest in Okinawa, but their actions suggest otherwise. If nothing else, they would love to drive the United States out of Okinawa. We were here to push back any aggression or Chinese contingencies. Hopefully, just our presence would do that. This is not like the jungles or mountains in Tajikistan; it was more like a police action or crowd control in a public square.

I was not a huge fan of this type of military maneuver; neither was Sam. I spoke to Captain Johnson about the rules of engagement in what looked like the beginning of a military coup. He told me it was just like any conflict; if fired upon, return fire. I asked him if he had ever been in a combat situation that took place in working society. He told me it was all the same and part of being a soldier. He told me we would love Fujan, known for its tea and everything they do with tea.

And he told me I was wrong about the mountains and forests; we will be setting up camp in the lush Jiulong Valley forest. I could not argue with him because I was out of my element here, but a military maneuver in a national park seemed inappropriate. As always when we set up camp, we set up a perimeter, and someone would take point at night. Sam took it usually, but our new leader wanted someone more experienced out front. He told Sam it was nothing personal, but we knew it was.

Sam went along and did what he was told. I did not feel this to be a threatening environment, but our captain had the experience. Nightfall in the forest is like a camping trip with the family; our captain wanted a cold camp so no fire. Just as well it was July and still hot even at night. Our unit was a little larger than I was used to; we had seventeen men.

Before this, I the most in one unit was seven. We had one man on point both front and rear. The rest of us laid down for some shut-eye. I woke sometime in the early dawn to whispering. Our captain and one other member of the unit were in conversation.

I sat up to see what was going on, but they ignored me and walked in the direction of where our point man was positioned. Sam was already there, and by his tone, I could tell he was not discussing the weather. When I got close enough, I could see a body on the ground. The captain was still ignoring me even after I asked what went on here. Sam spoke up and said that this idiot just capped a civilian.

Captain Johnson ordered Sam to keep silent. I said OK and asked who is this man lying on the ground. Our unit leader then ordered me to be silent. He then ordered us both to return to the others.

Sam said, "You cannot just ignore that your boy here shot a hiker. One man alone in the woods, unarmed, what the fuck were you thinking?"

Captain Johnson said we do not know who or why this guy is here, but our point man is given permission to eliminate anyone he feels is a threat. Sam said that is what you are doing right now, removing my brother and me because we are a threat. He told me to take Sam and return to camp. and that was a direct order. No one talked about the incident again, and I assumed they buried the guy in a shallow grave, a casualty of war. But the more I got to know our new captain, the more concerns I had.

Sam had not said another word, but his body language suggested to me that the pot was boiling. When we came to the city of Fujan, I thought we would keep an exceptionally low profile, but our captain had other ideas. He was acting like a college kid on spring break. He and his men took to the first bar and put down their weapons outside, and it was like Mardi Gras. Sam looked at me and wondered what happened to the Marines; were we on vacation or did we still have a job to do, the job we enlisted and took an oath to do?

He told me he was looking around and would be back. I could not bring myself to join the others, so I just waited outside. Feeling like a lost man, I wondered if the next three years would be like this one. Sam came back after about fifteen minutes and told me a foreign military truck was on the way to this area. I went inside the bar to find our captain, but his men said he had gone upstairs with one of the local girls.

I said, "Are you fuckin' kidding me. There is a militia on the way here, and I do not think it is to get a beer."

One of the men asked me how I knew this, and I responded by telling him my point man; my brother was doing his job. This man did not appreciate my tone and told me to get my brother on a leash. I lost my cool and took a big swing that landed right on his nose.

Sam had my back and asked if anyone else wanted a piece. Just as we were about to come to agreement, shots were fired. It sounded like they were coming from inside the building. One of the men said that is our captain he is a man of many talents.

I said, "Yes, but who was he firing at?"

Just at that moment, shots fired into the building. Civilians were in the line of fire. I tried to direct them to the upstairs, but they panicked and started to fall like as if they were in a video game.

I ordered the men to open fire at the front door. Sam had gone outside and taken an elevated position; he fired upon the first vehicle taking out the driver. The second pulled in behind, and Sam took out two more gunmen. Now the men had a chance to take position outside and forced the resurgents to retreat. At least, I thought they were resurgents.

When the smoke cleared, there were twenty-one civilians dead on the floor. The rest were alive but wounded; what a fuckin' mess! Captain Johnson came down the stairs still tucking his shirt in and applauded. He told us excellent work.

I looked at him and asked, "Work? This is a massacre and one that should never have happened."

He said, "We stopped the resurgence, didn't we?"

I told him, "This is not the Marines I signed up for, and this is not what soldiers do. We could have taken this fight away from civilians, or just maybe there is no fight at all."

He told me that he had heard I was a little soft.

Sam came into the room and asked, "Where these guys got their training? You want to call me undisciplined, fine; you want to put me in line, make me a heel hound? Fine, but you call my brother soft again, I am going to show you."

Before Sam could finish, the captain said, "Show me what? I heard you think you are a badass. Let us do this boy; I am going to teach you the lesson someone with balls should have taught you a long time ago."

He told his men to clear a little room and get out of the way. I told him to rethink this because my brother does not play. He told me he was the golden gloves champion back in New York, four years in a row.

Sam put his weapon down and took off his jacket. Captain Johnson walked up to him and took a big swing; Sam moved out of the way and then sent a left hook to the captain's jaw that rocked him. The captain felt it but took another swing that was wild and way off the mark. Sam measured him and then hit him square on the jaw with a deadly right hook. The captain's eyes rolled back in his head as he slammed to the floor.

Someone in the crowd said holy shit. I heard, 'This guy could hit but that was some Mike Tyson shit'.

I made a sign of the cross and said, "Oh, Dio, Abbi, Pieta, Di Me." Sarcastically, "of course."

We returned to the US Ronald Regan where Commander Anderson requested both Sam and I to come to his office. I wondered where the axe was going to fall on this one. He told us Captain Johnson was being reassigned. He told us his kind are still of use, but the chemistry of the unit had been compromised. He reprimanded Sam for striking a superior officer, but under the circumstances, instead of charges, Captain Johnson was transferred to another unit.

He told us we both were commissioned to a higher rank. I was now Captain William Calloway, and Sam was first lieutenant.

And said, "The remainder of your tour will be here in Okinawa. You will report to Camp Gonsalves immediately. That is all, dismissed."

I could not go without asking about the dead civilians. The commander replied that they were an unfortunate causality of war. I could not accept that, nor could my brother. I felt formal charges should be brought against Captain Johnson. Sam told the commander that behavior is not what soldiers are about.

He replied, "You are not soldiers; you are Marines; and as such, you follow orders, sometimes shit goes sideways."

I asked about the dead civilians again and how the situation could have been better handled.

He told me it was war and that is an unfortunate byproduct.

I told him that it did not feel like war; it felt like a police action. In war, we know who the enemy is; this time we had no idea who were fighting or why.

If Captain Johnson does not take the first shot, we do not engage; those civilians might still be alive. The commander asked me if I had proof that Captain Johnson fired first. I told him not at this time, but I could. Before I could finish my sentence, the commander told us the matter was not our concern, and we were dismissed. Oh, one more thing, and he directed this at Sam, "No more fighting or tournaments on base, understood?"

Sam said, "Yes, sir."

Marines train every day when not deployed. Sam and I had a chance to talk. I watched my little brother grow into a man before my eyes and could not be prouder. He had filled out to a solid two hundred pounds of muscle on his six-foot frame. He was built like Dad but more than the physical part; it was how he carried himself.

Loners are misunderstood; they are not all introverts or unable to integrate into society. As was the case with Sam, he could find his place in a team or go alone. What he brought was exceptional grit, loyalty, the instincts of a bloodhound, and a sense of security. I wanted to tell him all these things now that we had time.

As usual, just as I was about to compliment him, he had to upstage me. He told me he watched me become a leader of men, and I did so with the unit's best interest, not for fame or rewards. He told me he would follow me anywhere, and he knew the rest of the men felt the same way. He laughed and told me even though I was a skinny runt. I was six feet two but only a buck eighty-five.

I had a swimmer's body. Dad always told me I could have been the next Michael Phelps. I had to take this opportunity to address the Rambo stuff. I told him that Dad and I talked about it, but I wanted his take on the matter. He looked at me funny and wondered why I did not just ask him.

I said OK then, and asked him if he had a death wish. He sighed deeply and began to tell me a story. He asked if I remember the woman that hit our mom. I snapped at him because how could I ever forget?

I told him, "I remember you went up to her, and it looked like you wanted to watch her die."

He said that was not it; he wanted to make sure she could never hurt anyone else again. He told me he was not a monster. He did not enjoy watching people suffer, but he had to know she was gone.

He asked me if I remembered the mission in Nepal. I did.

I said, "I remember you killed three rebels and then stood in a standoff with the last one, waiting for him to go for his weapon."

He said I was wrong again; his gun jammed, and if he kept pulling the trigger, he risked a backfire.

So he acted like he was giving the rebel a chance, but he was giving himself a chance. He told me he reached for his knife with one hand as the rebel went for his gun. I interrupted and told him he could wait for us. He told me they were about to kill a prisoner; he did not know how much time he had. He continued and told me there is a difference between a throwing knife and a hunting knife.

He pulled his lucky throwing knife from the boot sheath he had made. He told me a knife with a handle is not meant for throwing because the back end is heavier than the blade end.

He told me, "From five feet you could stick the hunting knife any time you wanted. Because it does not have the time or distance to rotate end over end. A throwing knife is balanced, but I did not have the time to get to it. I threw the hunting knife and hoped for the best. I was lucky. I was twenty-five feet from that dude."

I asked again about standing over the man, but now I knew the answer. He had to make sure the guy was no longer a threat. I get it now. I told him Dad's theory about how watching Mom die had somehow made him immune to fear.

He told me that I was the one that needed all the answers, but he did not. We changed the subject to life after our tour. I did not think I could go right into practicing law even with Dad. He agreed. He told me the world is wide open for a man of my intelligence, and whatever I decided to do, he knew I would be the best.

I told him I was considering law enforcement. I asked him what he wanted to do, and without hesitation, he told me he was going to have his own exotic knife store. Maybe make his own someday. I could see that.

Even though Sam was ordered not to fight anymore in camp, that did not mean he could not find a tournament off base. In fact, he told me he had heard about this Japanese dude that was unbeatable. Some guy from Kadena, and he had a huge following. They set up tournaments outside the city limits; no police or military personnel were invited.

I asked how he found out about the fight and how he planned to get in. He said he put the word out that an American could kick this guy's ass, and I am just going to show up. Once I find out where it is. I told him I was going with him because I do not like this arrangement.

Underground bare-knuckle fighting is the equivalent of a cock fight or pit bull going at it for money. You have shady characters making bets and side bets, and nobody polices the action. These are street fighters, and most of the crowd are criminals. Americans were not welcome in this arena because the locals were not happy about the military presence from the start.

Sam's plan was to challenge this Japanese fighter and hope he accepted. Just one problem neither of us spoke Japanese. The fights lasted if there were bets, but if no bets, then no fights.

The Japanese dude presented himself in the middle of the circle and showed his hand full of cash, or Yen. He waited, but no one stepped forward. He reached into his jacket pocket and grabbed another hand full of cash. The crowd went wild. He took his jacket off and threw the money on the ground.

Still, no one stepped forward. Sam could not take it anymore; he stepped forward. The crowd went silent. The chant of America, America, America rang through the air. The crowd now began to chant, Kyoufo. Kyoufu, Kyoufu.

Which I came to realize meant fear. Sam just stood there taking it all in with a smile. Kyoufu slowly walked up to him and spoke, but all we understood was American. He wanted to know where Sam's money was, but Sam pulled out the insides of his pockets to show he had no money. Kyoufu began to laugh, and the crowd got hostile.

Sam took off his shirt and drew a line in the dirt. No language barrier there. Kyoufu picked up the money and handed it to another man. This meant that he had accepted Sam's challenge. Massive surprise.

At this point, I was more nervous than ever. I was not worried about Sam losing, but when he wins, will get out of there alive. The two met in the middle and measured each other. Sam was thicker and taller. This guy had to have something going for him, and it did not take but a minute to see what that was, he fought dirty.

It is a stereotype to say all Orientals are proficient in martial arts, but in this case, it was accurate. Kyoufu had a variety of kicks that he displayed in the first seconds of the fight. The first kick caught Sam off guard and sent him down hard. He looked at me, and I just shrugged my shoulders in disbelief. Sam realized now this was a different kind of fight than he was used to; he must adjust.

As Kyoufu postured for the crowd, Sam approached him again; this time Kyoufu sent a foot right at Sam's face. Sam ducked and sent a sharp right jab to the Japanese fighter's groin. This sent him to his knees in agony. Sam asked me how you say we are even now in Japanese. I did not know.

The crowd was stunned and quiet. I know now we are in trouble when this is over. Kyoufu got up and made a throat-slashing gesture to the crowd. This guy was quite the actor. Sam approached him again with a mock gesture of touching fists just to play the crowd himself.

Kyoufu bowed slightly and began another series of misplaced kicks. Sam moved out of the way and waited for another opening. When it came, he delivered a short-left hook and then a right to the abdomen. Kyoufu doubled over in pain. It looked like this guy had never been hit before.

Sam knew it was over and just waited for him to get up. When he did, Sam hit him with his best right hook to the jaw. Game over. Kyoufu was out. Some of the men from the crowd came over and helped him up, all the while giving us the evil eye.

They stood him up in front of the man that was holding the money. I did not believe my eyes as to what was happening and cried out to stop, but it was too late. This man sliced Kyoufu's throat, and they let him drop to the ground. He looked over at Sam and me holding up the money. I do not know what just happened.

The crowd quickly began to disperse. The man lay on the ground surrounded by his own blood. We went to him, but it was just a matter of minutes before he was dead. Sam told me there must be more honor in death than in losing to these people. We did not know what to say or do; I made the sign of the cross and said, "Oh Dio, Abbi, pieta di me."

That is my default setting. Sam recited a verse our mom read to us on many occasions, "Whoever dwells in the shelter of the Most High will rest in the shadow of the Almighty. I will say of the Lord, 'He is my refuge and my fortress, my God, in whom I trust'." The soldier's prayer.

I was the kind of person who had to process the events of my life, long after they happen. I clearly remember the beginning and the end; it is the in-between things I struggled to retain. Sam and I had finished our tour of duty and were now flying home. It seemed to me only yesterday we enlisted, only yesterday we learned of the political side of war. As usual, Sam was sleeping, but I had too many thoughts swimming around in my head.

I wrote to my dad many times and told him of my struggles. He supported any decision, but what I needed was to hear it aloud. I woke Sam and told him I had decided. He told me he made one too, he was going back to sleep. I told him to give me a minute, and he did, grudgingly.

I told him I was applying to the FBI. He told me he already knew. I asked how. He said that I wasn't the only one that wrote to Dad. I told my brother that the things we witnessed, the injustices, the brutality, the barbaric, and the inhumane made my decision easy. I told him I needed to make a difference, and even though I love the small-town atmosphere of Warm Springs, the people, family, friends, and, of course, Dad, I needed something more.

I thought Sam was asleep again, but he turned to me and said that I needed answers. I agreed. He told me he wasn't sure if all questions had answers. Why people do the evil they do, makes no sense, but they do.

He said he did not believe even if you ask these people that they know, but you go on brother and ask anyway. I asked him if he would continue fighting. He told me if there was a fight, he would be there because he needed to know. I asked what he needed to know.

He told me he needed to know if that guy is better, that is all. Simple. I went on to describe how it felt to serve and walk in our dad's footsteps and a bunch of other emotional stuff, but Sam was asleep, again.

Dad picked us up at Camp Lejeune; he looked tired and lost a few pounds. He was semiretired and spending much of his free time helping fellow veterans. Twenty-five percent of veterans that saw combat have PTSD. Most of us that served and returned whole feel guilt of some kind.

Our brothers that did not return or those that were disabled in some way never escaped our thoughts. But for the grace of God go I. Our dad was trying to gauge the amount of emotional distress Sam and I had suffered. My letters were vague, but my journal that l left with him after our first leave was not. I was the emotional one, and sometimes, getting things out is better than holding them in, like my brother.

Sam had displayed moments of rage and a total lack of fear, but he always found a way to cope. I still wrote from time to time. Dad told us if we needed to talk about anything, he was ready to listen. I asked him if that meant he would open up about his time in the Raiders. He laughed and said he was ready to listen not talk.

He then asked us what we wanted to do first when we got home. It was unanimous, pizza from Big Joe's. The ride home was about six hours, and of course, Sam fell asleep. Dad knew from my letter that I was making a career change. I told him the same thing I told Sam on the plane.

I needed to make a difference. Dad told me that with my military service, my law degree, and my 179 IQ, the application process should be a slam dunk. That is phase 1; phase 2 is field training. Richmond, Virginia, the field office for the FBI was only a two-and-a-half-hour drive from Warm Springs on Highway 64. Serendipity, but first, home and a 24 cut Big Joe's with pepperoni and mushrooms.

The house was exactly like we left it; nothing had changed. It was if Mom was still here. Dad said there was no reason to change anything. Sam and I agreed. We all dug into that pizza as if we had never eaten before, and talked small into the wee hours of the morning. It was so good to be home.

The months would fly by now. I was working in the field as a special agent. SA Calloway. Sam's dream of owning an exotic knife shop was becoming a reality. He started out of Dad's garage but now rented a storefront. Dad still spent most of his time with the veterans, but when he was not, he was at Sam's shop.

They had become close now like he and Mom were. My first case was a suspected homicide in Pennsylvania. A young girl whose body has not yet been found. Believed to be the victim of her drug-dealing boyfriend. Little evidence and the witnesses' stories were inconsistent. Sounds like a perfect first case.

The few witnesses were more like nosey neighbors, all with their own theories on the crime and victim. The one constant in the story was the lake where the body might have been deposited, along with the murder weapon. A knife. The local police were not equipped with a diving team or forensics unit.

We were called in to coordinate with them. Despite a noticeable inflection in their voices, the Derry police were just like the police back in Warm Springs. Helpful but limited. Because of the amount of time that has passed since the actual crime was committed, this case would be difficult for anyone to piece together. The accused in this case was serving a five-year stretch for possession, distribution, and owning a gun, which is a parole violation.

At least, he would be easy to find. Allegheny County jail in Pittsburgh, about an hour from Derry. The accused in this case is Jason Ford from Derry who believed he was set up and soon his lawyer would have him back on the streets. I introduced myself as SA Calloway, and my partner was SSA Connie Tibarius, an FBI veteran of ten years. Jason was a conspiracy theorist; he swore he would never harm his girlfriend whom he intended to marry someday.

I informed him that we were dragging the lake and witnesses put him in the area where the girl disappeared. This evidence would ensure that he served the maximum of the five-year sentence. He continued to declare his innocence and that there was so much more to the story. I showed him a picture of the missing girl; she was seventeen at the time of her disappearance. I wanted to see his reaction.

He never flinched, either he did not know this girl or did not have any feelings for her whatsoever. He put his head down for a moment and then repeated his earlier statement that there is much more to the story. SSA Tibarius was satisfied with the interview and called for the guard to let us out of the room. She told me he was guilty, and the body would be found in the lake. I was not so sure.

When we returned to the Derry police station, the rest of our team was shaking hands and thanking the locals for their support. Our team was led by SSA Neil Pendercost who had twenty years of experience in the field. SSA Kellen

Smith, Patrick Willis our computer tech, and Daniel Level our liaison, we just called him the mouth. Connie and I rode together, while Neil rode with Kellen, Daniel, and Patrick.

I asked Neil why we were done here, and he just said it is in the hands of the local and state police now. Something about the case did not feel right to me, and I voiced my opinions to SSA Tibarius. She told me not to get too caught up in solving every mystery; we did our job, and now it is on to the next case.

After a case, I liked to make the two-and-a-half-hour drive to Warm Springs; the drive cleared my head, and I missed my brother and Dad. I had an apartment in Richmond, but it just was not home yet. The weekends, I would spend time with my family. Sam's knife shop was about a mile from the house in Warm Springs. I stopped in hoping to catch my dad there as well.

Sam always asked me if I was eating enough. I told him I was a bachelor, so of course I am not eating enough. I told him he must be still working out because he looked like he put on another twenty pounds of muscle. Sam and Dad both liked their free weights, and Sam had a heavy bag out back of his shop. I never cared much for weight lifting; I was a cardio kind of guy.

He went to the mini-fridge and grabbed us both a drink. When he handed me the drink, I noticed his knuckles were red and scabbed. I asked if the bag did that or was, he fighting again. He ignored the question and told me to look at the new knife he was working on: a thirteen-inch Kukri made from Damascus steel.

He had become an expert bladesmith, and I was so proud to see the passion he had for his craft. He made the forge himself, and the online orders were pouring in. I told him I knew the shop would be a success. He had a birthday coming up, on November 24th. He would be 25, and I the old man of 30. I asked him if he wanted to see a game, and get some wings.

He said sure if I was in town, and had time. I told him I always had time for my brother. He then showed me the back room where he had targets set up. He reached down and pulled his lucky throwing knife out and hit the bull's-eye on the first try. I smiled and told him that is why it is your lucky knife.

I asked him if Dad was here today, and he told me he was, but he went home because he was not feeling well. He said he thought he might have the flu; it was going around. He told me to stop over at the house and check in on him. I said I would and told him I loved him.

He said, "I know."

As I stepped out of Sam's shop, my phone went off, the director of our field office; she told me to meet up with SSA Tibarius and head to West Virginia. We would be briefed by the state police in Grafton. It was about a three-hour drive from Warm Springs, and I would not have time to see my dad. The rest of the team was already there when Connie and I arrived. Our liaison will be filling us in on the details of the case.

Three teenagers, two boys, and one girl have all gone missing in the last month. All three were students from Bridgeport High School and lived in the Bridgeport area. Jason Hall, 14, a freshman was the first to be abducted; he was reported missing on October 19th. The second is Scott Anthony, 15, also a freshman; he was reported missing on

October 23rd. The third is Tiffany Jameson, 13, an eighth grader, and she was reported missing on November 12th.

A video was sent to the parents of Jason Hall, the first boy taken, an email with a link to the video; it was sent two days ago on November 20th. SA Patrick Willis, our computer technician, set up the video for us to view. I was taken back to Nepal for a second and had to refocus. The victim's hands were tied above his head; his head was covered with a hood.

His feet were left untied. The unsub was careful not to show his face as he poked the victim with what we assumed was a cattle prod. He then ripped the shirt off the victim to reveal previous marks left by days of abuse. The victim kicked wildly in obvious pain as the unsub continued the assault. Then the unsub lifted the hood to show that it indeed was Jason Hall.

The unsub kept his back to the camera and then demanded $50,000 be delivered to a yet undisclosed location. He then warned about police involvement. Patrick would now attempt to trace the email's origin and reexamine the video for any identifying information. He and Daniel, our liaison officer, would remain with the West Virginia state police while Neil and Kellen went to Bridgeport School to interview the principal.

SSA Tibarius and I were on to Jason Hall's house to talk to his parents. I could not imagine the pain something like this could cause for a parent, and extracting information from someone so distraught was not easy. SSA Tibarius took the lead because of her experience, and I observed. She told them everything in our power was being done to ensure the safe return of their son Jason. She asked the Halls if they had noticed anyone unusual or out of place in the neighborhood recently.

Mrs. Hall was overcome with grief and could not speak, so Mr. Hall answered all the questions. He said no there was not anyone that he noticed. Connie asked if there was new construction in the area or cable installations. Salespeople or anyone asking for donations?

Mr. Hall said no, but then Mrs. Hall remembered they were having problems with the Internet service and called the provider. SSA Tibarius asked if someone came to the house. Mrs. Hall told her they did, and a man came into the house to look at the modem.

Mrs. Hall began to unravel again thinking she let the man into her house that took their son. Connie assured her that was not likely and that we were done for today. She asked if Jason had a laptop, and if we could see it. Mr. Hall said of course. SSA Tibarius assured the Halls we would give it to our technician to see if Jason had been contacted by anyone online. Mr. Hall was ready to go to the bank and get the money.

I told him, "We would have a uniformed officer stay at the house and wait with them for the call; until then, try to get some rest. I know how difficult this is for you, and I am deeply sorry for what you are going through."

Outside I felt compelled to ask Connie why we did not get more information. She felt it best to allow the Halls to calm down. I told her if that was my son, I am not going to be calm until I get him back. Connie told me we could take the laptop to Patrick and then look up the Internet provider in the area and see what their procedures are for modems that are not working properly. She said she thought all that stuff was done online these days. Why did a tech have to come out? She told me to reach out to Neil and Kellen and have them talk to the parents of the other two children that were abducted, to see if they had Internet problems as well.

On the way to check out the Internet provider, we were informed by Patrick that the video of Jason Hall made its way to social media. Neil and Kellen interviewed the parents of Scott Anthony and Tiffany Jameson. There was no Internet technician that visited their homes, no apparent connection between the three children except they all went to the same school. They all rode the bus but not the same bus.

There were no sporting events, school activities, or even common friends. These kids did not even know each other. So what was the common thread? How do three children get abducted in broad daylight in a busy school with hundreds of potential witnesses?

Neil and Kellen were going back to the school to talk with the principal again. SSA Tibarius and I arrived at the Comcast building and went in to talk with the Internet provider. I took the lead on this and introduced myself and agent Tibarius. I asked who the tech was that serviced the residence of Mr. Joseph Hall at 111 Hallow Way in early October of this year.

The receptionist guided us to a tech working at his desk. He told us that night it was Eric Stroud, and he took out the old modem, replacing it with a new one. I asked if it was common for the modems to go bad. He said it happens a good bit, but it is an easy fix, and we do not charge the customer.

I asked if they ever subcontract with independent installers. He said no; it is all done by Comcast. However, the modems are sold sometimes to E-Waste systems; they refurbish cable boxes, modems, cell phones, etc. Then sell them to independent contractors. It is big business for tech geeks.

I asked where an E-Waste system could be found in the area. He said, "There is one close to here," and he looked up the address for us. "But and you did not hear this from me, a lot of the guys that work here never turn in the old equipment, they sell it and pocket the money. As I said, it is big business."

I asked if we could talk to Eric Stroud.

The tech said, "Do not bother. I know the guy everyone goes to cause he pays cash. His name is Tyler Koenig."

I asked for an address.

I connected with Patrick on the way to Tyler Koenig's residence. SSA Tibarius asked if there was any personal information that could be retrieved from an old modem. He said you could get an email address and then with the use of a VPN or Virtual Private Network, you could send untraceable emails. We were starting to piece together some vital information. Just say our guy here, Tyler buys an old modem and then resells the equipment to a private contractor or installs it himself.

That would explain the emails sent to the parents. But we do not know how he could abduct all three from the same area and not be seen. Maybe Tyler can answer that question. His house was near Bridgeport School; he could have been watching and waiting. Pulling up to the curb outside the Koenig residence, it did not appear anyone was home until a gray panel van pulled into the driveway.

We got out and asked if this man was Tyler Koenig. He told us his name was Tyler Rhodes. I told him he fit the description of a man named Tyler Koenig. He told me to get the hell off his property. I introduced myself and agent Tibarius.

He remained belligerent and arrogant. I told him we just had a few questions about his business. He told us it was none of our business, to get a warrant and come back. Otherwise, he had nothing to say. I asked him if he was aware that three children had been taken from Bridgeport School, and as I continued, he started toward me. A big man, all of 6'4" and 300 pounds. He stopped just short of me and said again, "Get the hell off my property."

We left but told him we would be back.

I asked Connie if she had ever encountered such hostility. She told me everyone watches television and thinks they are lawyers. It is common. Even though we did not get a good look at the man in the video, he was a big man. She agreed.

Her phone went off; it was SA Pendercost; the unsub had contacted the Halls and set up a drop site for the ransom. He also told us that emails were sent to the parents of Scott Anthony and Tiffany Jameson with videos. We were en route to the Halls' residence, but I could not help mention that because of the recent videos we are running out of time for Jason Hall. Connie agreed.

Mr. Hall was to make the drop; he had the money in a briefcase. He would wear a wire, and we would be watching from a distance. The drop was an old high school, in the back on the steps to the rear entrance. A rundown neighborhood, an abandoned school, dimly lit area. Perfect for an exchange, or Mr. Hall could be a target.

We wanted to use an agent, but the unsub was watching and knew what Mr. Hall looked like. We insisted on a vest, and he agreed. We set up a perimeter and surveillance. I asked Connie how many of these drops she has been involved with in her career. She told me too many, and the prognosis was about 50%.

Most unsubs are not equipped to hold their victims for extended periods of time. Kidnappers are rarely as organized as you see on TV; they are usually desperate for money. Now this guy is different; he is a psychopath; the videos suggest a level of malevolence and narcissism. Which means he has no compassion for his victims that does not bode well for recovery.

Mr. Hall approached the rear of the building and the bottom of the steps; it was dark, but he could see a box at the top of the stairs. I had a bad feeling. I ordered him to stop, but he continued up the steps to the box. I ordered him again and then got out of the car. Connie ran after me, and the rest of the unit followed.

We arrived at the scene as Mr. Hall was down on his knees crying out in agony. He had lifted the lid on the box and found his son's head inside. I turned to SSA Pendercost and told him this is not about money; this guy enjoys the pain he is causing these families; we better find the other two kids fast.

This was a defining moment for me; it took me back to my days in the field as a Marine. The slaughter of innocent women and children, the barbaric behavior, the senselessness of it all. I had to hold back my emotions and focus. We went back to what we know so far, and all roads led to another visit to Tyler Koenig. The team met at the state police barracks in Grafton to piece together the information we had gathered.

The unsub had personal information on all three of the victim's families. He had access to the children without causing suspicion. He had a private place to hold the children. He is not motivated by money. Thinking aloud, I asked how someone could go onto school property without being noticed. They would be regulars or have permission to be there; security in the school today is tight. A bus driver, a delivery driver, school supplies, food, repair people.

I told SSA Pendercost that Connie and I were going back to the school and talk to the principal one more time. There is something we are missing. Principal Elaine Morris was in her office and still in a state of flux over the three missing children. She assured us that she told the other members of our team everything she knew. I noticed there were flowers on her desk and a card.

I asked about them. She told us the Social Media Club started a Teacher of the Month contest about a year ago. I asked how that worked. She said the members of the club handed out ballots at the beginning of every month for the students to vote on a teacher or faculty member that went above and beyond. We were given choices of prizes and gifts from the local shops in the area.

I really like the idea. She told us she was honored last month and chose flowers from Lois's Flowers and Gifts in Bridgeport. I asked who brought the flowers. She said they were delivered. On a hunch, I asked her if she had a new Internet service installed lately.

She confirmed that new modems were installed throughout the school in the spring. Including the one in her office. I thanked her for her time and gave her my card if she needed us for anything. Then I asked if our tech guy could come by, and check out the equipment. She agreed but wondered why.

I told her it was standard procedure. Outside the school, I looked around; it was dismissal and the amount of people and chaos. A florist's delivery truck could come and go without anyone even asking questions, but taking a particular person, even in this crowd, would require patience and skill. It is just the first available child; it does not matter to the unsub. A crime of convenience or opportunity.

How would he know about the order unless he worked at one of the florists? Principal Morris mentioned that the contest started last year and that the winner was given a choice of prizes. Connie told me that the Social Media Club posts all their activities. I mean that is what social media is all about, so anyone could monitor the events. But the unsub would have to know exactly what was being delivered and when, or just take a huge chance and hope for the best.

Let's stop by Lois's Flowers and Gifts. Lois told us she had an order from the school, but it was months ago, not last month. She showed us her records to confirm. I thanked her for her time. On the way back to meet up with our team, I wondered what Patrick would find; could the school's routers and modems have listening devices? And what about the parents of the abducted children, any connections we overlooked?

Money was not a factor even though the unsub asked for ransom but $50k is not a lot of money.

Even if all three parents paid the $50k, that is not a great sum of money; it hardly seems worth all the trouble. SSA Tibarius told me the guy is trying to inflict as much pain and suffering as possible on the parents; he is just using the kids to do it. The money is arbitrary. OK so, why these people then? Were they just surrogates?

One other theory we did not discuss is that this guy is just getting started; he is sloppy but smart enough to avoid leaving an obvious trail. He is figuring things out as he goes. Evolving. This is him learning, so it is far from over unless we catch him. Patrick was calling. I asked him what he found.

He told me that all the modems in the school had been bugged with listening devices and cameras. A transmit wiretap was connected to a wire with a microphone and a tiny eye or Wi-Fi spy camera. He said it was quite sophisticated but easy to spot with a sweep. I looked at Connie, and we both agreed it was time to visit Tyler Koenig or Rhodes again. We arrived at the barracks to inform Neil of our intentions; he informed us we were done here and headed home to the Richmond office.

I was stunned and asked why; we were close on this one. He told me that it was the order from the director; there is another case in Ohio. We will be briefed in Springfield. I was furious; I wanted to see this through; I wanted to bring the children home to their parents; I wanted this sick bastard off the streets and behind bars where he belongs. So that was it; we just packed up and left after the hours and days we put into this case, the effort, and now someone else would come in and take over.

Neil told me to calm down that this is not television and said, "We don't catch the bad guy in an hour. We don't always watch the villain taken away in cuffs." He understood my compassion for the families involved but you can't let personal feelings dictate your actions. "You must put this one behind you and move on to the next case."

I told him I could not shut off my feelings like that, and I did not know how he or anyone else could.

He told me, "Years and years of practice. Let's go."

It took some time and many miles for me to put behind the case in Grafton. Because of her experience, Connie was a tremendous help. She told me she was the same way when she started; her first year in the field was a huge revelation.

She recalled a case of a missing wife in Texas, "The woman was a wife and mother of three, but one day, she disappears. The husband calls the police, and they look for her for three days. We were called in and the evidence pointed to the husband, but before we could connect the dots, we were called to another case."

I asked if they ever found the woman.

She said, "No and the husband then killed the three children. He's serving life in prison, and we had the evidence to start a case against him, but after we left, the state police never followed up. They were treated like a runaway; the woman just left her family and took off. I keep my emotions in check now."

I agreed and asked what she had on the new case. She told me there were four missing adults: three women:

Ashley Gordon, 34, from Springfield; Judith Morning, 23, from Columbus; Sharon Elizabeth, 29, from the Dayton area, and one male, Jordan Lewan, 21, also from the Dayton area.

As I began to ask if there were any commonalities with the victims, her phone rang. We were informed that the bodies of the first two victims, Ashley Gordon and Judith Morning, were found. It looks like we have a serial killer in Ohio.

The Springfield police had put together a map of the Springfield, Columbus, and Dayton area. The victims were from upper-class neighborhoods. The police had information on the victims and their families, and a partial profile could be put together. Probably a white male in his late 20s or early thirties with access to the victims in some capacity. Whether it be personal or professional.

SSA Tibarius and I went to the coroner's office to inspect the bodies of Ashley Gordon and Judith Morning. Both victims were found in a dumpster behind a prominent restaurant in Columbus. I told Connie that dumping the bodies in a busy city is either arrogant or foolish.

She said, "Or desperate. The unsub would have to be a strong man; these victims were not small. Both were large women. To lift them up and throw them in would normally take two men, maybe three."

I agreed. I asked if there could be an accomplice.

She said serial killers normally work alone, but it is not out of the question. Both victims had multiple bruises, contusions, and lacerations. They were bound for days without food or water or allowed to use the bathroom.

I asked the coroner what was the cause of death She said blunt force trauma to the head and lifted one of the victim's heads to show the mark. Probably a baseball bat.

SSAs Pendercost and Smith went to Columbus to interview the family of Judith Morning. Ashley, the young wife of the city's comptroller for the State Senate. Marvin Gordon, 42, held the position for the last two years. Judith Morning, the daughter of State Legislator Peter Morning. Meanwhile, our liaison, Daniel, and our tech Patrick were to speak with State Treasurer Margret Elizabeth of Dayton, the mother of Sharon.

We were on the way to speak with State Legislator Casper Lewan, the father of Jordan. It was clear now that our unsub was targeting these victims for a reason. Since no attempt was made by the unsub to contact the victims' families, we could assume that Sharon Elizabeth and Jordan Lewan would meet the same fate as Ashley Gordon and Judith Morning.

What we gathered from our time with the victims' families is that all of them left the house at the same time and were not seen in the company of anyone new or unfamiliar. All the victims had routines for the day on which they were abducted, so someone could have been watching. We met with the Springfield police to confirm the information on Ashley Gordon's abduction. They took me and Connie to the area where Ashley might have been taken, while the rest of the team was on the way back to Springfield.

My phone was going off, and the name was Bath Community Hospital. I was informed that my father was ill, and they could not reach Samuel Calloway. They could not go into specifics on the phone, but I needed to come to the hospital. I told them I was about four hours away, and I wasn't sure about the policy for leaving in the middle of a case. But I would be there as soon as possible.

I told my team my father was in the hospital, and they all told me to go. Be careful and let them know about my father. I told them I would.

The drive to Warm Springs seemed like an eternity. Alone my mind wandered from my father's health to the case in West Virginia and back to my father. Then the case in Ohio. I could not explain it at the time, but my instincts told me there was a connection. It's funny how time can stand still and fly by at the same time.

Pictures and images of my dad, Mom, Sam. Memories both good and bad, how my life unfolded, and how it would not be this way if not for my dad. He was the rock, the foundation this family was built on. His strength, Mom's will, Sam's enduring loyalty. That was what this family was about. I could not imagine my life without my dad or my brother.

I tried to call Sam, but he never answered, doubt he even carried his cell phone. Bath Community Hospital, I was here. In the lobby, I asked for Thomas Calloway.

The receptionist told me, "Oncology is on the 3rd floor, and Mr. Calloway is in room 311."

The elevator door opened, and I could see my brother and several veterans I have met over the years. Dad's friends. Sam stood up, and I gave him a huge hug. Sam, not much on hugs or any kind of emotional display, just let me, as always. He told me our dad had stage 4 lung cancer.

He's had it for a while now; just never told us, or anyone. I asked if he had seen him yet; he said no he was waiting for me. The doctor came in and asked for Will and Sam; we stepped forward. He told us the cancer was advanced, non-squamous, or non-small cell lung cancer. The checkpoint inhibitor, pembrolizumba, has not been as effective as he had hoped.

We interrupted and asked if we could see our father. The doctor said for a minute. I was already tearing up. Sam put his hand on my shoulder and gently pushed me toward the room. I have never seen our dad so vulnerable, always the picture of health and strength.

Fuckin' cancer. When he saw us, he perked up and put on a good front. The first thing he said was to Sam. He told him he got a letter from a Notification Officer yesterday; you lost your dog tags, and you are now listed as MIA. He had a stern look on his face as he told Sam to get it straightened out.

He struggled to sit up as he told us to come closer. I told him whatever he needed I would get for him. The words that followed would stay imprinted in my mind forever. Our dad told us a story of his time with the Marine Raiders. Sam and I stood there riveted to every word.

It was the first and only time our father talked about his tour of duty. The story gave us a whole new perspective on our dad and the man we thought we knew. It made our tour seem like a picnic. This man had seen and experienced a horror like no other and lived to tell his sons. I was speechless; how could he live through that and be the kind of man we knew? Our mom knew and raised kids together.

This man was always my hero, but now I saw him in a different light. He had become God-like. I was humbled. He finished by telling us our mom was the strength of our family, and we both should find a woman like her. And said, "The good lord has chosen to take me now and I can only hope to be reunited with her, so I can tell her what great sons she raised."

He pushed himself up and saluted us.

"William and Samuel Calloway, I was proud to be your father. Always be there for each other; you are both destined for remarkable things." Those were the last words our father said to us.

I cried; Sam recited the soldier's prayer: "Oh Dio, Abbi. pieta, di me."

A military funeral was something to behold; the honor and ceremony were breathtaking. Once a Marine, always a Marine. I shook many hands and saluted many Marines. Sam did what Sam does. He stood alone by the grave site, reciting verses from the Bible. Others walked by and acknowledged him, but he stayed focused on the task.

That was my little brother; he had a strength about him that was equal parts to our mother and our dad. It was like they gave him the best both had to offer. He was my rock now although I would not tell him that. I was on bereavement leave for a couple of weeks and grew anxious to get back to my team. I had no contact with the bureau except for condolences and flowers.

I would need to check in with the director shortly, but first I needed a heart-to-heart with my brother. It has been a long, strange trip for us since we were kids. Five years younger than me, but he never acted like a younger brother.

He and I were polar opposites when it came to emotions or for that matter anything else. He loved being alone and did not talk much.

But the time had come for me to connect with my brother. I asked him if he was OK, and what his plans were from here. He looked me dead in the eyes and told me that I needed to find a good woman and raise a family. He told me I was always meant for important things professionally, but the one thing that I was destined for was to be a father, and not just any father but the same kind of man our dad had been.

He told me I was cut from the same cloth. He told me William Calloway was his hero but to stop looking for all the answers.

And said, "Try to accept the things you cannot change, speak for those that can't speak, reach the unreachable. Teach the unteachable, right the wrong, protect the weak. Then go home, put down the badge, and be a father; that's where your greatness lies. Now that our mother and Dad are gone you are the best person I know."

Then he saluted me. Tears filled my eyes as I returned the salute and told him I loved him.

He said, "I know."

Director Sullivan waited for me in her office. She stood and offered me her sympathies.

I thanked her and then asked where we were on the case in Ohio.

She looked at me and told me my team was headed to Pennsylvania. I asked again about the case in Ohio. She told me that case was turned over to the local police. The case in Pennsylvania involving a man serving time and a body dumped in a lake had taken a turn and my team was already there.

The suspect, Jason Ford, was released because the evidence had gone missing. I told her I remembered the case; our team was responsible for dragging the lake and the forensics. She assured me my team was not responsible for the missing evidence.

I asked how the evidence went missing. The weapon was recovered from the lake and had Ford's prints on it. But no body was found. We interviewed him to let him know we found the weapon hoping for a confession. The director knew we did not get a confession but asked me anyway. I told her what the suspect told us and there was something in his body language to suggest he was telling the truth.

The director asked me if I was taking the words of a drug dealer, and murderer. A prisoner will say or do anything to be set free. If I had more experience in the field, I would know that.

Something came over me at this point, I began to raise my voice, and that was not like me. I have never been disrespectful to a superior. I do not know if it was the events of the past week or just my overall frustration with the politics of law enforcement. I told her it seemed like we were just janitors for the local police. We come in, clean things up, and hand over the evidence. Time to move on now. And asked, "Is this the new FBI, or am I missing something?"

Director Sullivan was patient with me because of what I had been through, but she suggested that I was not ready to come back to work yet. I lost my cool, and told her I don't know if I ever started to work here yet. She then told me it was not a request but to take a week off and get my head straight. She said she would notify my team.

I left her office not knowing if I had a career or where I was going. My first thought was my dad would be so disappointed in me; he would have told me I should be smarter than that. I didn't want to stay in Richmond for the week, so I headed for Warm Springs. The drive would help me clear my mind. I'm not a drinker, but I stopped at a bar just outside of Richmond.

As I sat down at the bar, my phone went off; it was SSA Tibarius, and she was concerned about me. She told me the bureau needs good people like me, to keep positive and come back to work soon. I really needed that; she's a good person and a hell of an agent.

As I said, I'm not a drinker; this was my first beer in years. I sipped on it and took in the local atmosphere. The bartender came over and asked me if I wanted something particular on the television; they had four televisions. The one in front of me had the news on; I did not even notice when I sat down.

It was eleven o'clock on a Monday morning, and few people were in the place. November in any state was election time, and politics was the topic of the moment. A topic I always avoided, but the two guys sitting down at the bar a few chairs from me were totally engaged.

They noticed me and realized they had not seen me here before. They asked where I was from because I was wearing a suit; I did not look local. I politely declined the conversation and returned my attention to the news. They were talking about the governor of Pennsylvania, Governor Rhodes.

The men once again directed the conversation my way. I knew now they were too interested to let this go, so I had to produce a story that explained why I was in this bar, and it could not be that I was suspended from the FBI. I bought the men a drink and slid down to talk to them. I told them I just lost my job at the bank for writing too many bad loans. I could not go home to the wife just yet. They were taken by that story, and it was like we had been friends for years.

They had many opinions on the topic of politics, especially the dirt. I asked about the governor because his face was on the television screen as we spoke. The first thing I noticed was he was a big man, 6'4" at least and three hundred pounds. or more. One of the men told me he played college football at WVU as an offensive lineman.

He didn't start, but it got him a free ride through college. He went on to say, "ol' Joseph Rhodes had a fondness for the ladies, especially the working kind. If you know what I mean. Rumor has it he spent most nights chasing strippers and doing drugs. That would be why he never cracked the starting lineup."

Scandal after scandal in school, and that followed him into his married life and his early political career. Still balls deep in scandals but always comes out smelling like a rose.

I told the bartender to keep them coming. These boys were just getting started. The other man decided to chime in and said these were not rumors but facts. Governor Rhodes got an exotic dancer pregnant; she had his kid, but the governor paid her off, and it never affected his career.

My instincts were on full alert, and some of the missing pieces of the puzzle were coming together. I still had no tangible evidence, but it was time to get out of this bar. I pretended to get a phone call from my last job and excused myself. I put a twenty down on the bar and thanked the men for their company.

They wished me good luck and told me they would be right here if I came back. I had no doubt about that. My next stop was Warm Springs to see my brother. I texted SSA Tibarius, but no answer yet.

I could see the sign for Warm Springs up ahead, and I got a text from Connie. I pulled off the road to look. She told me I was being sent to my Alma Mater, Harvard, to speak on law enforcement opportunities. I thought it was a joke considering I was questioning that very thing right now. She assured me it was legitimate, and it was the director's way of gauging my attitude and compliance.

To see if I was ready to be a team player again. She urged me to take the opportunity for what it was and get back to the team ASAP. I thanked her for the heads up, but this was not good news. I pulled into the driveway of my home, my childhood home. The only home I have known.

I had to collect my thoughts before I called Sam, even though I knew he wouldn't answer. I was at a crossroads in my life and my career. I needed answers, but I wasn't even sure what the questions were. I wanted to make a difference not be part of a machine. I was not in a good place.

Sam and I could always talk. I took a ride over to his place. With very few words, my brother could center me, balance me, and set me straight. My younger brother. His exotic knife shop had excelled, and he had become an excellent knife smith. He had a passion for his craft, a passion for which I was now envious. I walked inside, and of course; he was around back throwing.

He looked up at me and asked what I was doing here on a Monday. I noticed a shiner on his eye and asked, foolheartedly, who she was, knowing already he was fighting again. I had to give my opinion on the world of bare-knuckle fighting even though he would not care to hear. I knew the kind of people that gathered for those events and reminded him of Okinawa. These fights were all about gambling, and people die if bets are not covered. Win or lose you can end up on the wrong end of a gun.

Bad people brother. He told me the fights help with the rage. It takes over sometimes, and I don't know what else to do with it. I told him he still needed to look death in the eye. He asked me if I really believed that bullshit. I noticed he still carried the knife Dad gave him; I asked if he still had the lucky one in his boot.

He laughed and said he would be buried with both. This was life according to Sam, and his simple nature always put things in perspective for me. My younger brother. He needed to know now why I was here and what was bothering me. I told him in not so many words about my crisis.

Everything I believe in is being challenged, everything I work for, every job I start, every case I throw myself into was turning to shit. I told him I might be done with the FBI. Maybe I will start my own law practice today. He asked me if that was my decision, and he supported it, but don't give up on the FBI yet. When we were in the jungle, things never went as planned and I always found a way.

I told him he had a lot to do with that; he told me he would always be here for me. He told me it looked like shit went sideways again, but I would figure it out. I tend to let my emotions get in the way. Sam agreed but said, "Your emotions are also what gives you the passion to do what few people can do. In short, brother, look past the forest, and you will see the tree."

I gave my brother a hug and told him I loved him.

He said, "I know."

I stopped in to see Director Sullivan, and she wasted no time informing me of my next assignment.

She was watching my face to see if I was back, or if I still had some rebellion in me. A big thanks to SSA Tibarius; without her warning, I could have walked into another confrontation. I thanked the director for the chance to speak at my Alma Mater and left her office. This was a chance for me to refocus on my career and why I got into this line of work. This was a good thing.

Flashbacks to my youth, football, and Emily my first real love. Campus life is where bright young minds are molded by brilliant old minds. I loved it. This was also bittersweet; Mom and Dad were both legacies at Harvard. The name Calloway still meant something in these halls. I walked up the steps to the lobby and asked the receptionist for the president of the university.

I told her SA William Caloway to see him. The president was in a meeting, but the dean of admissions would see me. Neither the president nor the dean was here when I was in school. I was flattered though when the dean knew me without introducing myself. He knew of my parents as well, and we sat in his office and talked for hours. About college life, the Crimson (football team), law, and just life.

It was just what I needed. When we were done, he asked me if I needed to freshen up before speaking. I told him I was good to go, feeling refreshed by the conversation. The auditorium was packed, and I must admit I was a little nervous. Once I took the stage and got behind the microphone I felt at home.

The two hours flew by, and before I knew it, I was telling the crowded room that I saw the future here and it looked bright. I know, a little corny. After shaking many hands, I was approached by a young lady who introduced herself as Julie Mullen, a senior journalism major, who was quite inquisitive.

She was originally from California where her father was a law professor at UCLA. Her mother was a photographer for the *Los Angeles Times*. They moved to Massachusetts because Harvard offered father tenure. Her mom was taking pictures for the *Cape Cod Times* now.

I asked what path she was following. She told me she was working on a book but hadn't ruled out a career in the news industry. I asked what the book was about. She told me it focused on the government and the trickle-down effect of the economy and the crime rate in America.

She asked me if I thought it was a coincidence that a poor economy leads to higher crime. The government's answer is to increase the police force, but they have no budget for the increase. Before I could answer she went into a rant about the corruption in politics. I had to get out of there fast. I knew I was in a fight I could not win.

I told her a flat-out lie. I told her politics has nothing to do with law enforcement. Ironic because that was the very thing that had me so frustrated. She was persistent and explained to me that her uncle was a uniformed police officer in Los Angeles and politics played into every scenario. She told me he and his partner grew frustrated by the number of times they pulled off cases just as they were ready to make an arrest.

How many times they worked with the FBI, and they were pulled off the case before an arrest. Her statements hit home on so many levels, but I could not discuss our process with anyone outside of law enforcement, especially not a member of the public. I excused myself and handed her my card. In retrospect, I should not have done that, but it was just a force of habit.

The dean of admissions and the president of the university came by to thank me and see me out. They could not say enough good things about my mother and father, even though they never met. It did my heart good to hear these things about the two people that molded me into the man I am today. I needed to be reminded of what a great foundation my parents built for me and continue to live up to it every day.

I thanked them for the opportunity and headed for my car. I checked my phone, and there were three messages, one from the director and two from SSA Pendercost, the leader of our team. I was to go to Derry, Pennsylvania, and meet up with my team. I ignored the message from the director for now.

Jason Ford, the suspect in the case of the missing girl, was assumed to be dead, but the body was not found yet. The murder weapon was found when we dragged the lake, and his prints were on the weapon. He was released from the Allegheny State Prison after serving two years of a five-year sentence. The weapon went missing from the evidence locker at the Derry police station. Now Jason was on the loose and had abducted two more women. Both of whom were witnesses that we interviewed.

I met up with my team in Derry; it felt so good to be back. The Pennsylvania state police were collaborating with the local police. Getting up to speed, the local police told us that Jason Ford was a regular at an establishment called Queenies, a topless bar close to the lake where the victim was allegedly dumped. Jason was a small-time drug dealer with a taste for the dancers at Queenies.

The victim, Wanda Williams, was a dancer at Queenies. She and Jason were seen together on many occasions. Jason would deal out of Queenies with the dancers, his biggest customers. Queenie was known for dealing as much as serving alcohol, and when Jason started to get the bulk of her clientele, Queenie made his and Wanda's lives hell.

They had an argument one night, and Jason let it be known he had a gun. We believe Queenie was the one who turned him in for carrying an illegal firearm. With his priors, he would serve five years at least. That was about the time Wanda quit Queenie, and then she went missing.

I had to ask how a felony gun charge was only five years. In my experience that would carry a ten-year sentence and a hefty fine. The team would split up now with me and Connie going to talk to Queenie. I told SSA Tibarius that it is well-known in this area that Queenie deals and she is a smart woman.

Smart enough to do what she does for years without being shut down. Queenie knew her patrons and would hire any woman willing to take her clothes off. Mostly local girls, down on their luck, strung out on something, and willing to do anything for a paycheck. It is rumored that Queenie is a made woman with connections. She paid her girls cash so there would be no paper trail, and most of the girls did not even have a bank account.

It kept them off her books too. In talking with her, I got the feeling she was pretending to be dumb and care about the people in this town. I knew better. I asked her if there was any truth to the rumor that she had high-end dancers called into her place when she had special customers. She said all her customers were special.

I asked her again if she had high-priced dancers come to her place, and go upstairs with senators, governors, and even vice presidents on the campaign trail. She laughed and said that people will always talk shit.

We left knowing no more than when we went in, but SSA Tibarius was wondering where I was going with that line of questioning. I told her Queenie had a room upstairs, and my guess is she hired girls specifically for the nights when her customers wanted privacy and discretion. She would not get big money for the girls she hired in the bar downstairs; they were not good enough for governors or mayors that passed by here on their way to Pittsburgh.

She realized these men would pay top dollar, and she had to find the type of girls that would fit the need. There was a funeral home across the street from her place. You could park an Escalade there for hours, and no one would notice. Connie told me that was good police work and added that she bet the two girls abducted by Jason Ford were dancers as well. It fits his MO. I told her Queenie was no help, but if you talk to her regulars, they will know something.

We waited outside for a while until a man came out, and we stopped him. He said he didn't want any trouble, and we assured him there would be none. We asked if he knew Jason Ford, and he laughed, saying everyone knows 'ol snowball. I assumed that nickname was because of his drug dealing.

The man laughed again and said, "It's not because he throws them. Jason loves his blow and his hoes if you know what I mean."

I said, "Yes."

He continued, "He took Sunshine and Pixie just to piss off Queenie."

I asked if those girls were dancers. He said yes, but no one stays here long, cannot make any real money. Once Queenie takes her cut. Most of these girls work here just for a fix; they can't stay straight, and after a month or two she gets rid of them, or they just stop coming to work.

I asked about Wanda Williams.

He said he remembered her; he remembered seeing her with Jason. If a girl here hooks up with Jason, you never see them again.

I asked what that meant.

He said, "That is all I know."

When we met up with the rest of our team at the Derry police station, I was about to fill them in on my theory about Queenie and the room upstairs. But the focus was on Jason Ford and where he had taken the two girls.

Daniel and Patrick had reestablished communication with the neighbors around the lake. While SSAs Smith and

Pendercost inspected the suspects' last known residence. Connie, and I took a drive down route 30, the major highway in the area.

I could not let go of the connection; the connection Queenie's place had with this case. Thinking aloud I wondered where you would go to get high-priced exotic dancers, discreetly. The Internet was too obvious and traceable; sometime, the old-fashioned way is the best way.

Connie told me she was with me, but I had better make this connection soon because our job is to find Jason Ford. She told me she trusted my instincts, and I was a good agent but right now I had better tow the company line. I agreed and told her this would only take a minute to indulge me.

I pulled into a restaurant/bar named Sharky's, a lovely place.

I told Connie, "you would be surprised by the information that can be obtained from people in a bar."

I told her to wait five minutes and then follow me into the restaurant. I took off my suit jacket and tie so as not to look like a fed.

Left my gun and badge in the car. It was almost one o'clock in the afternoon on a Friday, a nice crowd. I stepped into the bar, and the bartender asked what I would have. Not being a drinker, I had to pretend to look for something different. I asked about their draft beers, and she went on for what seemed like an eternity about the numerous types they served. I just told her to give me the only one I remembered.

I scanned the place for something or someone, but I knew this was a long shot. Next, I noticed Connie come in and sit on the other side of the bar, and it looked like she was going through the same process I was. I had to engage the bartender in conversation; she was very willing. I told her I sold cars for a living, and my brother was getting married. I told her I was in charge of the bachelor party, and I needed to get some girls, dancers, you know strippers for the party.

She said, "That's nice."

I told her that I had heard that mayors, governors, senators, and even vice presidents came through here on the campaign trail.

She said she didn't know about that, but the Pittsburgh Steelers visited when they were in camp at St. Vincent University.

I said I loved football.

But the conversation wasn't going where I needed, so I went for broke. I asked her if she knew where I could get strippers for the party. She said no and left to wait on someone else. I was on duty, so I never touched my beer and threw a $10 bill on the bar.

Just as was about to leave a man sat down beside me and asked if I liked the beer. I told him it was fine, but I had to get going. I noticed Connie got up and left the bar. He asked what I did for a living and if he could buy me something I would like. I told him I was on the mayor's congressional staff and duty calls. He said OK but if the mayor comes through this way, give me a call, and he handed me his card. Bingo.

I asked him if this was discreet.

He said, "Absolutely and we have nothing but the best if you know what I mean."

I said, "I do, and thanks, I'll be in touch."

When I got back to the car, Connie was waiting for me with the look I have come to know as concerned. She wanted to know when I was going to let her in; on what angle I was working. I told her that it all may sound like a reach, but what if the missing girl in the lake was a cover-up?

Jason Ford is a low life, no doubt, but he frequented Queenies and knew all the dirt on her side business. The high-end escorts hired for political figures. What if he had some evidence, some hard evidence of the illegal activities at Queenies? Wouldn't you think Ford is the type to try and cash in on the evidence?

She asked me if I thought he had the balls to blackmail a government official.

I said I think he might, and if he had video evidence, he would ask for a lot of money.

She asked me how the girl, Wanda Williams, figured into my theory.

I told her Wanda and Ford were involved, and I believe that someone had her killed and framed Ford for the crime. This way he's behind bars until he gives up the evidence.

She asked why not just kill Ford and the girl.

I told her that they probably couldn't find the evidence and didn't want to take the chance that Ford gave it to some else to hold. They want that evidence, and this is some sick chess match to see when Ford will give it up.

She told me the evidence is the only thing keeping Ford alive.

I agreed. That evidence could end careers.

Connie asked why we haven't found the body yet.

I told her this was part of the chess match. They put Ford away on minimal charges hoping he caves and gives up the evidence, but he doesn't. If the body turns up, the forensics could actually clear Ford, but he doesn't know that. So he sits in jail for two years and has had enough. He is willing to turn over the evidence if they agree to let him live.

I told her it sounded weak in my head but now that I have said it aloud it has some merit.

Connie told me it was not a reach; it sounds like you are on to something. That is great police work, but we both know they will kill Ford if he gives up the evidence.

I agreed, so we had better find him soon.

She asked me about the two girls he took with him; were they willing participants in this deadly game?

I told her that Ford probably told the girls he was about to come into some big money, and they were dumb enough to believe him, just like Wanda Williams.

Connie asked who would reduce the sentence for Ford and let him out early. Someone made the judge look at new evidence in the case, someone like a governor. Ford had a public defender, and they would not bother with an appeal. No, this came from a higher office.

I told her we better check in with the team. When we got to Derry police station, I could tell something was about to happen. We were met by SSA Pendercost, and he told us they found Jason Ford in Jeanette, about forty minutes from here. He was dead, an overdose. They found the two girls with him, also dead, and the badly decomposed body of Wanda Williams. I thought he was joking.

I told him to get a forensics team out to the scene and said, "Let's go."

He told us we were done here; the state police would take over.

I asked, "How that was even possible? How do you suppose a body that was missing for a year shows up in a house in Jeanette? How did Ford get released from prison, and why?"

Connie stepped in and pulled me to the side. She reminded me that this is the job sometimes, and I needed to show some professionalism in front of the local police.

I was livid and had to go outside to cool off. I picked up my phone and called my brother. To my surprise, he answered. I asked him what he was doing. He told me he was on his way to West Virginia. I asked why; he told me it was best I did not know.

I said OK because I knew what that meant and asked if we could meet somewhere.

He said, "Sure, when?"

I told him I was leaving Pennsylvania shortly and would text him in an hour.

I asked SSA Tibarius if she would mind riding with Neil, and Kellen, that I had business in West Virginia. She gave me that look but agreed. I told her I would see her in Richmond tomorrow.

I took Route 30 to 79 and would be in West Virginia in two hours. I texted Sam to see if he could meet me in Fairmont. He responded, and that was a surprise.

He asked, "Where?"

He was in Smithfield, close to Fairmont. I told him to find a bar and let me know the name and address. He agreed. I met up with my brother at Benny's at 1122 Fairmont Ave. in Fairmont.

He was in the parking lot standing beside an old RV. I asked if it was his new ride. He said it was his home away from home. I assumed it was for when he went on the road to fight. Sam wasn't much on hotels. I would ask about the fight, but I knew he would avoid the questions knowing I did not approve.

He wanted to know why I wasn't working, and I wanted to know how I was able to get him on the phone. He told me he kept his phone with him on the road to check on his online orders for the knife shop. He told me business never sleeps. He could tell there was something going on and told me to spill it. I knew Sam had no patience for bullshit, so I got right to the point.

I told him about the case I was just on in Pennsylvania and how it was connected to a serial killer in West Virginia. I told him I had no tangible evidence, but I knew it in my gut. He told me he always trusted my instincts.

I told him this guy, Tyler Koenig, is responsible for the kidnapping, torture, and murder of three high school teenagers from the Bridgeport area. Sam said that is close to here. I told him there is a connection to the abductions and murders in Ohio as well, but I cannot prove that either.

Sam told me that I was the law, go track 'em down.

I told him it is not that simple; we are not on those cases anymore. I have no authority.

Sam asked what he could do to help.

I asked him if he remembered Nepal and Tajikistan.

He did.

I told him in war it is 'kill' or 'be killed', no rules other than to survive. It was a level playing field. We knew the enemy was evil, and we could be just as evil if necessary.

Sam stopped me and told me what I was about to say. I told him I had to play by the rules, but the criminals do not; the red tape and politics kept me from doing my job. Sounds like Okinawa. I told him I felt helpless.

Sam asked again what he could do to help.

I reminded of how many times he told me I should settle down with a good woman and raise a family.

He told me, "That was my true calling."

He remembered. I asked him what he would do if one of my children was abducted.

Sam stopped and looked me dead in the eyes with a purpose on his face. He told me I knew exactly what he would do. I would track down this motherfucker and end him. No questions asked.

I asked about the law.

He told me the SOB that took my children was not concerned about the law.

"Why should I be?" he asked me one more time what I wanted him to do.

I told him to keep an eye on Tyler Koenig for a couple of days. I knew he was our guy, and he was far from done. He was developing his skill as a killer, and I knew he had a taste for it now. It had been a few weeks since the bodies of the missing children were found. He was getting anxious to get back out. I knew it.

Sam asked if I had an address. I did. I told him to just observe, not to contact, and to keep in constant contact with me. I handed him a disposable phone, so there would be no connection with me.

He laughed and reminded me that as far as the Western world is concerned, he was MIA because of his missing dog tags. He told me he was a ghost. "Oorah. Oorah, brother."

The team would take routes 70 to 95 to FBI headquarters in Richmond. I was in no hurry to get to the paperwork that would be waiting for me. I took a detour to Warm Springs. I had to see my childhood home and maybe spend the night there before heading to Richmond in the morning. On the way, my phone went off; it was a number I did not recognize. I answered; it was Julie Mullen. She asked if I remembered meeting her at Harvard University.

I told her I did, but I did not have time to talk. Of course, I did. It was three and a half hours to Warm Springs. She was insistent we speak, and I could use some company right now, so I indulged her. She told me she had gathered information on a case involving the governor of Pennsylvania. I asked what information.

She told me that when Governor Rhodes was lieutenant governor, he had frequented a place called Queenies in Derry, Pennsylvania. I was listening. She told me her sources informed her that the lieutenant governor had a longstanding relationship with an exotic dancer named Elizabeth Koenig. She went on to say that Elizabeth became pregnant during the governor's election campaign. Still listening.

Mr. Rhodes was married and could not risk the scandal, so he bought Elizabeth a house in West Virginia and sent money regularly to ensure her silence. I asked how a writer comes by this kind of information. I told her she was acting like an investigative reporter, not a writer. She reminded me that her career options were wide open.

I asked her why she was not in school. She told me she graduated early. Getting back to the information she obtained, I reminded her that it was against regulations for an FBI agent to discuss any information involving ongoing investigations.

She said she understood and went on to say that twenty-five years ago, Elizabeth Koenig gave birth to twin boys. There are no records of the birth in West Virginia; they were born in Ohio.

I sat up in my seat and took notice of this information. But I had to stop Julie there and ask where she got her information. She declined to comment because a good journalist does not reveal her sources until the book is published. I had to end the call, but she insisted we meet at some point soon. I did not respond.

After spending the night in my own bed for once, I could not help but be impressed by the information Julie had obtained. No one from our office would give out that information, so she must have gotten it from the local police or canvased a large area of three states and interviewed many people. Either way, that was good police work, and it validated my suspicions. But our team was not on the case, so it was on to Richmond and the next case.

The director pulled me into her office first thing upon my arrival. She reminded me of the enormous amount of paperwork waiting for me. She then asked me if I knew Julie Mullen. I was surprised even though I should not have been. I told her that she was a young journalist major I met at Harvard when I lectured.

She had a stern look on her face when she told me Julie had called the bureau wanting to talk to her. I had to confess that I gave her my card at the lecture, and I should not have. She told me there was no harm done but reminded me of the protocol. I agreed.

She told me to have Patrick or Daniel speak with her and give her the usual rhetoric that we give to all reporters. I assured her I would, and then she informed me of a new case in New Orleans, but first to get to the paperwork from the last case. I agreed and left the room.

Sam drove his old RV into Bridgeport and found a spot to park. It was morning in West Virginia, and he needed some breakfast. The diner was open, and he could smell the eggs and bacon from the parking lot. Sam could blend in anywhere, and he did not want to have the look of someone out of place, someone people would remember if asked. He was quiet and polite as he ordered the breakfast special, two eggs, three strips of bacon and hash browns, and a glass of orange juice.

He casually looked around the place, but nothing caught his eye. He finished and paid the check. He looked at the address I gave him and drove past the house to see if he could park somewhere out of sight to observe. It was not easy to find a spot for an RV in the immediate area. He parked in an empty lot at the end of the dead-end street.

The house was just barely in view. He decided to take a nap. For Sam, a nap was fifteen minutes, and when he woke, he noticed a gray van leaving the driveway of the house he was watching. He texted me and asked if Tyler Koenig was a big dude that drove a gray van.

I texted back and affirmed that. He did not respond. He instead followed the van from a distance. Sam was the only person in the world I trusted, and he would carry on as if he were on orders. I loved that about my brother.

Our team was headed to New Orleans to assist local police with a case involving threats and vandalism in both abandoned and active churches. We met at the bureau's office outside of Zion City, home to six churches. New Orleans had a thin police force in this area, and the bureau felt that some unfamiliar faces would be able to obtain more useful information. The religious groups in the area are very guarded when it comes to law enforcement. Right now, everyone was on edge because of the violence projected on a place of God.

Just as we arrived, a bomb threat was called in at an abandoned church. The bomb squad diffused it before any harm, but the threat appeared real. It was C4, plastic explosives, but just enough to get some attention, not enough to cause extensive damage. It did not escape my attention that my focus on this case was pronounced. I had turned a corner. The call let us know where the bomb was, and the bomb itself was a minor threat in an abandoned church.

What was the message? The media was all over the story now, giving our unsub or unsub's plenty of attention. My gut was telling me this was a diversion; my team was investigating antireligious groups, atheists, antisocial groups, mock terrorists looking to make a political statement using religion as the platform.

Sam followed Tyler in his gray van to a gated community. He noticed that Tyler stopped at the gate and put a magnetic sign on both sides of the van. He could not read the signs. The gate opened, and Tyler drove inside. The gate closed.

Sam waited, waited for an hour until the van returned. The gate opened. Tyler drove away. He headed out of town, and Sam followed. Giving the benefit of the doubt, Sam figured this man could not be so stupid as to abduct someone in broad daylight.

But he remembered what I told him about the high school abductions and continued to follow. Tyler drove to an old auction barn that looked like it was no longer in use. Just off the main road and down a long dirt road. Sam could not follow down the dirt road, so he parked just off the main road and walked to the barn keeping out of sight. Tyler stopped and opened the barn door wide enough to drive inside.

Sam approached the barn and crept around outside hoping to find a viewpoint. He found a man's door and gently, quietly opened it. He peaked around every corner until he spotted Tyler getting something out of the back of the van. It was something wrapped in a blanket. He sat it down on the ground and then proceeded to get the equipment out of the van. It looked like video equipment.

He found a chair and positioned it in front of the equipment. He then removed the blanket to reveal it to be a child. Hands and feet were tied, and a hood was over the head. He removed the hood; it was a boy, gagged. Sam did not need to see anymore, and he reached for his phone, but realized he had left it somewhere.

No time now; he had to do something fast. He called out, "Tyler Koenig."

Tyler was startled; he jumped and grabbed a baseball bat from the van. He demanded to know who was there. Sam called him by name again, but this time Tyler told him his name was Rhodes and who the fuck wanted to know.

Sam said who he was was not important.

Tyler asked him to step out and be seen.

Sam told him he did not want that. And said "Here is the deal. You walk out of here now, and I will let you live."

Tyler laughed and said, "You ain't no cop."

Sam said, "No Tyler, and I ain't no ten-year-old boy either."

Tyler slowly approached the sound of Sam's voice and began swinging the bat to intimidate him.

"OK, Tyler, we are done talking." Sam told the boy to close his eyes and keep them closed. He told him he did not want to see this.

Tyler said, "No keep 'em open, I'm gonna smash this asshole's head in like a melon."

Sam stepped out and walked toward Tyler, the big man. Tyler was still talking shit, but Sam was quiet. Tyler laughed and swung the bat with such force you could hear it break the wind. Sam moved in; Tyler swung again missing wildly. Sam sent a left hook that landed right on the big man's jaw; it rocked him.

He shook his head and gathered himself for another swing at Sam. He swung repeatedly and often, missing each time, and when he tired, Sam sent his left foot to the side of Tyler's knee; you could hear the ligaments pop. The big man went down in agony; he went to his knees still clutching the bat. Sam walked to the other side of him and kicked the bat out of his hands. He measured the big man and then sent a swift right hand to his temple.

It was over. He stood over him for a minute to be sure the big man was dead. He was. Sam made the sign of the cross and whispered, "Oh, Dio, Abbi Pieta Di Me."

He then realized the boy was still in the room. This was a tricky situation; he was supposed to observe not engage but shit went sideways. Now what?

"OK, kid, you can open your eyes now."

Sam took out his knife and cut the boy loose. He started looking for a cell phone.

He said, "Surely the big man had a phone; everyone has a phone."

He went over to the body and searched. He found it in Tyler's pants pocket.

"OK, kid, I'm going to call 911. Take the phone and stay on until the police get here."

The boy was so shaken he could not get the gag off his own mouth. Sam helped him, and the boy grabbed ahold of him and would not let go.

Sam said, "Listen to me, I must go, but you are safe here until the police arrive."

The boy asked about the big man.

Sam told him, "He is not a problem, and he is coming with me."

Sam asked what the boy's name was.

He said, "Benjamin, Benjamin Sanders." He said his dad was the mayor of Bridgeport.

Sam said, "That's great kid."

The phone is ringing. "Hello, 911, what's your emergency?"

The boy didn't know what to do.

Sam told him to start talking and not to stop until they got there.

"Goodbye," Benjamin.

The boy began to talk and cry, and Sam hated to leave but had to. He dragged the big man out of the building and into the brush. He got the RV, threw the body in the back, and drove out. As he got to the highway and headed away, he could see the lights flashing and hear the sirens. He knew the boy would be OK.

We received word that a priest was being held at gunpoint in front of the parishioners at the Church of the Nazarene in Zion City. I had a feeling there was more than one target; in fact, SSA Pendercost gave the order for the team to split up and take uniformed officers to each of the six churches in the four-block area of Zion City. SSA Tibarius and I went to the church where the priest was held at gunpoint. Much like the bomb in the abandoned church, we felt like this was a distraction from the real objective.

The bomb squad was on alert and ready if needed. Connie was given the task of talking to the person or persons inside the church. She asked what their demands were and wanted to know if an agent could enter the building to talk.

The person inside responded with something he must have written himself, "These eyes are of a tortured soul; they can cut like knives or make diamonds from coal. If it is an idiom, you seek or have you become one of the sheep. Listen carefully to the last words I will speak. I wear the dragon around my neck like a leash. I call upon the pale rider to command the beast. Adrentus Bestiae."

I recognized the last part; it was Latin for the coming of the beast. I told Connie I was going in; she wanted me to wait. I took her phone and introduced myself as I entered the church. I told the man I was unarmed and just came to talk. This man just wanted an audience.

As I walked toward the man, I could see he was indeed pointing a gun at the priest as he delivered the sermon. The unsub waved me forward and nudged the nervous priest to continue. As I walked toward the pulpit, I directed some of the parishioners to get up and walk out. The unsub did not object, so I kept it up until I got close. I scanned the room for another shooter but saw nothing.

The priest calmed with my presence and read from Romans 12:12: "I appeal to you therefore, brothers, by the mercies of God, to present your bodies as living sacrifice, holy and acceptable to God. Do not conform to this world but be transformed by the renewal of your mind."

The unsub turned his attention to me and told me I would be a witness. The unsub pointed his weapon at me, and I told him he did not need these people anymore. They began to get out of their seats, and all of them headed outside. In my headset, I could hear SSA Tibarius asking me if they should come in, but I did not answer. I couldn't. This was just another diversion, and I had to secure this location quickly.

SSA Pendercost spoke to me telling me they had apprehended a suspect with explosives. I approached the unsub and told him it was over; we had his partners in custody. He took his eyes off me for a second and pointed the gun at the priest's head. I pulled my back up piece and shot him. He fell harmlessly to the floor.

I told the priest to go now, but he wanted to stay to administer the last rights. I was OK with that until I noticed explosives on the ground behind the pulpit. I grabbed the priest by the hand and shoved him behind the first row of seats. The explosion rocked the building and sent debris flying over our heads, but we were alive. The bombs were only meant to kill the priests and the unsubs; the parishioners were to witness.

The same bombs were found in each of the six churches in Zion City. To understand the crime is to understand the perpetrator. These extremely sick people wanted to be martyrs. They felt if they died in the presence of a priest that would ensure thcy got into Heaven. The team was ready to call it a day. Connie told me it was good to have me back.

SSAs Pendercost and Smith just gave me the head nod. We all got into our vehicles for the long ride back to Richmond. I checked my phone, or I should say my dad's phone, that is the one I used to stay in contact with Sam. I had one message; it simply read, "Got him."

Sam stopped at a Unimart in Summersville, West Virginia. He needed gas for his RV and a drink. He didn't know where he was going right now, but he didn't want to be in West Virginia any longer.

As he filled his tank, he noticed an extremely nervous man get out of a pickup truck driven by a woman. The man fumbled about and acted like he had just done something wrong. Sam watched him go into the store and then noticed that the woman that was driving got out and peaked in the blacked-out windows of the cap on the bed of the truck.

He finished filling his RV and then went in to get a drink. The nervous man was still in the store looking more lost than he was outside. Sam observed the man as he picked a drink from the cooler that looked like something a kid would drink, not a man. He then picked up some candy and a roll of electric tape.

This seemed odd to Sam, and the man's behavior was even more odd. Sam bought his drink but kept one eye on the man. He watched him get into the truck, and they both drove off. He sat for a moment and decided to follow; he wasn't sure why. He kept his distance for a while as the truck traveled about ten miles before getting off the main road and onto a one-lane road.

Sam couldn't follow now, but his curiosity got the best of him, and what else did he have to do today? The one lane turned into a dirt road that led to a barn: a barn that someone still used because there was equipment outside the barn. Sam got close enough to see the man and woman get out of the truck and get something out of the back. They pulled a sack out of the back of the truck and went into the barn.

Sam got a little closer and used his phone to take a picture of the license plate, which he sent to me. He wanted to leave it at that, but something drew him closer. He went around back and found a door; he opened it and went inside. He found a spot where he could hear the two people talking and settled in. They were arguing.

When we got back to Richmond, Director Sullivan brought the whole team into her office. She told us we did some excellent work in New Orleans, but the reason she called us together was because she got word that a boy was taken from his home in Bridgeport, West Virginia yesterday morning. The boy was the ten-year-old son of the mayor of

Bridgeport, Kendall Sanders. We all wanted to know if they found him yet, or if we were on our way to West Virginia.

She paused and told us this is the story that she had heard. The suspect is Tyler Koenig, the same man SSA Tibarius and Calloway interviewed in connection with the abduction and murder of the three high school students earlier this month. She told us this is where it gets interesting. The boy, Benjamin Sanders, calls 911 on the suspect's phone. He swears he was kidnapped by a big man and brought to an auction barn, close to Bridgeport.

The boy swears another man came into the barn and beat up the big man. His words to the police, not mine. This other man gave him Tyler Koenig's phone after dialing 911, told the boy to stay on the phone until the police arrive, and then took the big man away. We all looked at each other in amazement, and I played along.

Sam heard the two arguing over the person they kidnapped. Apparently, when they took off the sack that was covering the person, it was the wrong person. The woman was furious and began calling the man every name in the book. Sam couldn't see the person, so he got a little closer. It appeared to be a young girl. Maybe 13.

The woman got louder, and now Sam could hear everything. She told the man he was the dumbest human being on the planet. She wanted to know how he could make such a mistake when she gave him a picture of the girl they wanted, and she looked nothing like this girl. She asked him what they were going to do now. The man said we take her back and get the right one.

She asked if he was fuckin' kidding. The girl had seen their faces now, and she did not want to go back to jail.

The man said he would take care of this one and then get the right one.

She said she was done with him, and he could deal with this shit. She was leaving.

The man told her not to go or else.

She asked, "Or else, what? You don't have the balls or the brains."

All Sam heard next was a shot as the woman came stumbling toward him. She fell just short of where he was and then looked up at him, her eyes rolled over and then closed. He knew that the girl would be next, but the man had a gun, and Sam only had his knife. Sam hollered out to the man hoping it would scare him enough to take off. He told him the police were on the way; just let the girl go and walk away.

The man asked, "Who was talking, show yourself."

Sam told him there was no need for anyone else to die today. Just walk away, and you can live. The man started slowly toward Sam's voice but never put the gun down. Sam told him it was his last chance all the while counting the steps and listening to his voice.

He was close enough. Sam stepped out and let the knife go; it stuck right in the man's throat. He gasped and choked and fired off two more shots that landed harmlessly in the wall. Then he slumped over on his knees. Sam walked over to him and turned him over, blood squirting from his neck. He looked into his eyes; there was no life left.

Once again, he was faced with dead bodies and a witness. The little girl was scared beyond anything Sam had seen before. He told her he was cutting her loose and everything would be OK. She did not respond. He told her he would get her a phone, but once again, his was probably in the RV.

So he searched both the woman and man for a phone. The woman had one, and he told the girl to call the police. He had to get two bodies out of that barn and into his RV. He came back to the barn, and the girl was still hysterical and unable to talk. Sam did the only thing he could now; he texted his brother from the woman's phone and told him to call the Summersville police. There's a barn off the main road, about ten miles from the Unimart; a girl needs help; explain later.

Connie and I had a chance to talk after the meeting with Director Sullivan. She wanted to know what I thought of this idea that a stranger saved the mayor's son from certain death. She asked me if it could be a partner that turned on the unsub, or we had a vigilante.

I told her, "A partnership that goes south is more likely and that many victims of these types of attacks, ones that experience severe trauma have been known to create images in their minds, imagination is a powerful thing. The mind wants to protect the body; it's called hypervigilance."

She told me she was aware of it but never encountered it or knew anyone who did. I told her that made much more sense than a vigilante. She asked what I thought of Tyler Koenig just disappearing. I told her it was not our case anymore, but if it were, I would be talking to his mother.

She said this is all interesting, but you are just not ready to tell me everything, are you? Asked what she meant, but she just gave me that look and went back to her desk.

I told her that I was done with my paperwork and I was heading home.

She waved. I decided I needed to make the drive to Warm Springs, and there I would wait for Sam. He had not responded to my texts since the one he sent me about the girl that needed the police in Summersville. I needed clarity about the Tyler Koenig thing, but Lord knows when I would hear from my brother.

The two-hour drive from Richmond to my childhood home always cleared my head, except this time my phone; it was Julie Mullen again. I answered. She was excited to tell me that she had found Tyler Koenig's mother in West Virginia. Carolyn Koenig was an exotic dancer that had an affair with the then-Lieutenant Governor Joseph Rhodes. The affair lasted for years until Carolyn became pregnant with twin boys: Tyler and Taylor.

The governor bought her a house in Charleston, where she raised the boys with the help of the governor's money. His family is filthy rich. She went on to say that Carolyn had drug problems all her life, and even with the governor's money, she had to sell her body to make ends meet. She was sexually abused on multiple occasions by the men who came to the house for sex. She never filed any charges, but the police were always at her house.

The boys were always in trouble with the law as well. Carolyn finally met a man who wanted her for more than her body; she and the boys moved to Ohio to live with him. But, as usual in Carolyn's life, the bad far outweighs the good. She could not stay clean, and her new man had enough. He told her to leave, but Taylor wanted to stay with the boyfriend while Tyler went with his mom, and they moved back into the house in Charleston, where she lives now.

I told her that was excellent work, but I still cannot comment on any ongoing investigation. She agreed and went on to tell me that Tyler Koenig went missing after an abduction went wrong. The mayor of Bridgeport's son was taken from his home two days ago. Tyler was the suspect in the case, but he disappeared, and after they spoke to the boy, he claimed that a man came in and fought with Tyler, then set him free. I asked her how she got that information because it sounds like media propaganda.

She assured me her sources were credible. I told her I was home and needed to get some rest. She told me she thought the man the boy was talking about was Taylor Koenig because the police found Tyler's phone and in it were several calls to his brother. I told her she needed to let the police handle it from here, but she insisted she was on her way to Ohio to talk to Carolyn's ex; his name is Kenneth Singleton, and he lives in Dayton. She hung up, and all I could think was that girl has more courage than common sense.

Every time I walked into the home where I was raised, I felt a sense of calm and security. I half expected to see my mother in the kitchen preparing a meal or my dad sitting in his lazy boy watching football. That is what every child wants to see, but I was a man now, and it just dawned on me that I have no home. This was a bridge to my past, and nothing has changed in the years.

The air smells the same, and it feels like I should know this place. Unfortunately, what made this my home was my mom and Dad, and they were gone. My apartment in Richmond was for convenience, but I never felt like it was home. I came to this house on the weekends to see my family. That is what made it my home.

I love this place, and Sam refuses to sell, but he won't stay here either. My mind was a clutter, and I could not help but think about Julie; she was a brave woman, but knowing her could end my career. I had to get some rest and settled on the couch for a nap. I would have to get up early in the morning to drive to Richmond. Hope I can get some sleep. It could not have been long when something told me to open my eyes.

Sam was standing over me; he asked why I was there. I got up to make coffee and collect my thoughts; it was 3:00 a.m. I asked what happened in West Virginia.

He told me he would wait for the coffee and let me wake up a little. Then he threw a wallet down on the table.

I asked who it belonged to.

A man no one will see again.

I opened the wallet, and the license belonged to Peter Jenkins from Pennsylvania.

He said, "I assumed this was the plate you asked me to run."

And said he was acting on a hunch and it paid off. He told me that I must be rubbing off on him. I asked where Peter Jenkins was now. He told me the whole story of Tyler Koenig Rhodes and the people who abducted the wrong girl and planned to kill her.

I asked, "People?"

He said there was a woman too. I asked again where these people were now.

He told me somewhere in the Elk River; no one would ever find them. I asked about the girl and if she saw him.

Because the boy he rescued told the police a story about a man that saved him. If the girl tells the same story, that could be a problem.

Sam told me there was little time or choice.

I agreed, but it still was a concern.

He asked me what now.

I told him I was going to work.

He told me there was more that he wasn't telling.

I told him about Julie and the possibility of a twin brother in Ohio committing the same crimes.

He asked about Julie.

I told him the story of how we met and how she had put together this case.

He asked if she was alone.

I told him, "Yes; I think she works alone."

He told me to forget about work and go to this woman.

I told him that she could ruin my career.

He told me, "It sounds like she's saving your career. She confirmed all your theories on the case; don't let your fear of commitment cloud your judgment."

I told him I had to go to work, but since he was here, I wanted his thoughts on the house.

He told me he was never selling the house, end of discussion.

I asked him where he was going now.

He didn't answer.

I told him I loved him.

He said, "I know, Oorah, brother. Oorah."

Sam left, and I jumped in the shower, but as always, my little brother spoke with clarity. I did not trust my instincts when it came to women or relationships since Emily. But I had a job to do, and that is where my focus would have to be. As I got ready to go out the door, I noticed a vehicle pulled into the driveway, it was SSA Tibarius. She walked with purpose.

I asked what brought her to my house and why she wasn't in Richmond.

She told me the team was on their way to indict the governor of Pennsylvania on felony charges. The charge was a conspiracy to commit murder.

I asked how and why.

She told me the evidence that I theorized Jason Ford possessed was accurate. She said the evidence was found by the local police at Jason Ford's home in Derry. She told me the best part was that Julie Mullen was the one that brought the idea of the evidence and the governor's involvement to light.

I asked how that was possible.

She told me the woman has a way about her, and she's good at her job.

I told her that's great let's get going.

She told me, "No that my job was to go to Julie before she gets hurt. She's a brave woman, more courageous than most, but she is in over her head, and it is only a matter of time before she asks the wrong questions to the wrong people or is in the wrong place at the wrong time. The team will cover for you; they are all aware of the situation."

I thanked her for her friendship and understanding.

She told me she had an address for Kenneth Singelton in Dayton Ohio and "That is where you will find Taylor Koenig Rhodes."

I told her the evidence against Governor Rhodes won't convict him.

She agreed, but it would ruin his career, and the people of Pennsylvania deserve to know the truth.

I agreed and went on my way but not before Connie had one more question.

She told me Tyler Koenig is still missing, and the very next day in Summersville, West Virginia, a young girl was abducted. An anonymous call to 911 led the police to where she was held but no signs of the person or persons who took her, and the girl told a similar story. The story of a man who came and saved her from the bad people.

She said, "That is odd."

I agreed and went on my way. I knew my brother, and I knew where he was going. He had a two-hour head start so I had to hustle. My concern for Julie's safety was a priority, so I took a chance and texted Sam the address. 116 Edison St., Dayton. He did not respond.

Julie knocked on the door at 116 Edison St. It was 5:30 in the morning. She did not expect anyone to answer, but this was such a bad neighborhood; she wanted to be as discreet as possible. The house looked abandoned, but then so did the whole block. Her curiosity was on overdrive; she could feel she was close to a hot story.

She went around to the back of the house to see if there were any signs of life. Nothing, but it was an old house; breaking in should not be hard; and in this neighborhood, who would notice? She pushed on the door to test it, and it moved. She pushed a little more, and it popped wide open. She cautiously stepped inside and looked for a light switch;

it was pitch black. No lights, no electricity; the refrigerator door was open; and the contents stunk up the whole room.

She used her cell phone for lighting. She wondered how anyone could live this way. Or did they live here? She thought she had the wrong address but was compelled to check out the rest of the house before giving up. She tried the basement first; the steps were all broken. She had to be incredibly careful.

She felt like she was in a real-life horror movie. It smelled like death in that basement as the hair stood up on the back of her neck. She did not know what she was looking for, but maybe this is where Taylor Rhodes kept his victims. Her fears now overrode her curiosity, and as she turned to head back up the broken, old steps she thought she caught a glimpse of something in the corner of the basement. She shined the light from her phone in the area and slowly walked toward the object.

Close enough, she was horrified to find a dead body. It looked like a man, but it was hard to be sure in the dark. This was more than she bargained for, and she turned to quickly exit the basement and this house of horrors. Her mind allowed for a brief synopsis of the situation; maybe the body was Kenneth Singelton, the boyfriend of Carolyn Koenig. Maybe it was one of Taylor's abductions.

She got to the kitchen and noticed a man standing in the doorway, He was big and ominous. She had to think quickly and made up a story about being with the electric company. The man did not speak. Instead, he charged her and began swinging wildly. She fought valiantly, but he was too strong and knocked her unconscious.

I was across the West Virginia state line when SSA Tibarius called, and told me there was an abduction in Ohio. State Senator Michael Stroyer called the police last night and told them his wife and daughter were supposed to meet him for dinner at seven but never showed up and no call. He hasn't seen or heard from them since yesterday afternoon. The police found their car a mile away from the restaurant, cell phones still in the car.

I asked her if the team was coming to Ohio.

She told me they were not invited yet, and the case in Pennsylvania was priority one.

I asked where they were last seen.

She said the Senator lives in Columbus, and the restaurant was nearby.

I told her this sounds like our boy.

"I'm about two hours from Dayton. I suspect that is where he is holding them; have the police meet me at his address," she affirmed.

I tried to call Sam but got no answer.

Sam arrived at 116 Edison St.; it was 6:15 in the morning. He went around the back of the house and noticed a car that did not belong in this neighborhood. He figured it was Julie's. He went inside and noticed the stench right away. It was a smell he knew all too well.

There was no sign of Julie, and as he turned to leave the house, a man was standing in the doorway. It was a neighbor with a baseball bat. Sam told him to put the bat down; he meant no harm. Sam asked the whereabouts of Taylor Koenig.

The man said he doesn't know Taylor Koenig; the dude that lives in this house is Taylor Rhodes.

Sam said, "OK, where is Taylor Rhodes?"

The man went on to say that Taylor Rhodes was a bad man. He told Sam that Taylor didn't think anyone knew what he did, but we do.

Sam asked what he did.

The neighbor said he was a thief; he stole my television, and he stole from everyone in the neighborhood. The neighbor told Sam that Taylor took all the stuff he stole and took it to his warehouse.

Sam asked if the man knew the address of the warehouse. The man told him it was West 2nd Street, close to the house. The man told Sam, "Taylor keeps all of that shit down there, and he thinks I don't know about it."

Sam thanked the man and headed for his RV.

The man told him as he was leaving that if he found a 60-inch flat screen down there that it was his and bring it back.

Sam agreed and drove away.

I got another call from Connie, and she told me the police in Dayton were given the information, but they had to wait for Senator Stroyer.

I asked, "Wait for what?"

She said that is all she knows.

I told her I was there, thanks.

Sam pulled into the parking lot of the dimly lit warehouse. He parked in plain sight this time, not seeing a reason to hide. He opened the door and crept inside. This place had not been used in years. He went further and found an opening, and a pickup truck parked inside.

He went over and felt the hood; it was still warm. There were stairs leading down; he followed a single light to a dark hallway. Up ahead was another light. It was then he could hear talking. He got closer and saw a man, a big man, and three women.

They were tied and gagged. The man was setting up equipment. This looked all too familiar to Sam. The big man picked up one of the women and hung her by her hands on a hook. Sam had seen enough; he hollered to the big man.

"Taylor Rhodes," he yelled.

The big man stopped and looked around.

Sam spoke again and told Taylor to leave the building now.

Taylor asked, "Who the fuck are you?"

Sam came out of the darkness and spoke to Taylor directly. He told the big man, "No one needs to die here today, so just leave, and no harm will come to him."

Taylor paused for a second, then took off running out the back.

Sam got to the women and untied them, directing them to the stairs. They were hysterical, even Julie, as he led them upstairs. Just as they were about to get to the first level, Taylor came out of nowhere and struck Sam in the head. All of them rolled back down the steps to the second level. The women were screaming, and Sam looked like he was unconscious.

The big man came down the steps and began kicking Sam repeatedly. Julie stood up and jumped on the big man; he grabbed her by the throat and began choking the life out of her.

The wife and daughter of Senator Stroyer looked on in horror. They begged him to stop, but he just kept on choking.

Julie looked all but gone when Sam got up, and sent a sharp right hand into the big man's back. The big man let Julie go and went after Sam again. He swung wildly at Sam's head and connected several times.

Sam took the shots and then delivered a left hook to Taylor's face.

The big man felt that hit, grabbed Sam, and began choking him.

Sam fought to get free, but the big man was strong, and Sam was hurt. Sam reached for his knife, but it must have fallen out in the fight. He gasped for air and then turned to the women and told them to close their eyes. Sam's eyes fluttered and then closed; he began to fall to his knees.

The big man loosened his grip; it was all but over.

Sam opened his eyes and smiled at the big man. Then he drove his lucky throwing knife into the lower jaw of Taylor Rhodes.

The knife went through his neck and into his mouth. The big man stumbled and gasped, then fell to the ground. Sam stood over him for a second. No life left. "Oh Dio, Abbi, Pieta Di Me."

Sam turned his attention to the women and directed them outside. He told them he would call 911.

Julie asked who he was and why he was there.

Sam said nothing, got into his RV, and drove away. Julie held the daughter and mother in her arms until I arrived. I told her the police were on their way, and I would wait with them. She told me a man saved them or they would all be dead.

She was overcome with grief and could not talk anymore. She just held tight to the two women; they were not letting her go. I went inside to find Taylor Rhodes dead on the floor. A knife in his throat, Sam's lucky knife.

I pulled it out and wiped it off; near to that area, I found his bone-handled straight knife. It was not like Sam to leave either of those behind. This will take some explaining, but for now, I will be covering for my brother. This is the only evidence that puts him at the scene.

On the way home, I tried to call Sam several times, but there was no answer. Typical.

Agent Tibarius called and asked if everything was OK.

I told her, "Fine for now, and we would talk at length later."

She said she looked forward to it, and she mentioned how brave Julie Mullen was, that kind of woman does not come along very often.

I told her, "Message received, thanks."

I was looking forward to a shower and bed. It was a long day. When I got home there was Sam's RV. I walked into the house, and there he was sitting in Dad's lazy boy. I handed him both knives he left behind and asked him if he was all right. He looked up at me and told me he was going back to the Marines.

I asked, "Why?"

He told me he was in a bad way with the big man. He thought it was over for a second, but then he heard Mom's voice. I looked at him thinking he was joking. He told me that Mom said, "Be strong, Marine."

He told me that gave him the strength to come out of a fucked situation.

I told him I can respect, that but if you are worried about this vigilante thing, it will not stick. I told him this was a win for everyone. Bad guys dead, victims recovered, and the police look like heroes.

He told me that we had to go outside the law to make things right, but his life made sense these last few days. His life made sense as a Marine. He told me that my life is here in the FBI and that I was a damn good agent.

He also told me, "Julie Mullen was ready to die for him and those two women that she didn't even know. That kind of courage and tenacity is rare, brother."

I said, "OK, you are the second person to tell me that today. I will call her."

He told me that made him happy, and he was going to sleep here tonight. The last time.

I told him that made me happy, and by the way, "You are the bravest, most loyal person I know; I was proud to serve with you and even prouder to call you, my brother."

Tears were falling like rain down my face as I told my brother I loved him.

Sam got up out of the chair, tears now falling from his eyes, and told me he loved me too. Oorah.

The End

Where do we go when the laws on which we depend,
Are practiced by lawless men.
Violence in my eyes,
Blood rains from the sky,
You have forsaken me, Jesus Christ.
For now, might will make it right,
Vengeance is mine.
Oh, Dio Abbi Pieta Di Me.

I am not good at talking about myself, I had hoped to remain anonymous throughout this process but I must open up a little. I am the product of a hard working Italian family from a small town in Pennsylvania. My father ran a bakery and my mother was a housewife, both things are obsolete today. I was not exceptional at anything as a youngster except getting into trouble. I continued that trend as an adult with two failed marriages and countless meaningless jobs. I wrote my first short story when I was 16, entitled *The Gunner*. It was about five pages long and very poorly written. Handwritten on paper no less. I never showed it to anyone. It's not that I was ashamed of writing, it was that I knew no one would be interested. After my second failed marriage I began writing again and this time I took it more seriously. A lifetime of mistakes and heartache gave me all the inspiration I needed. My first book, *Tales From Behind Your Wall Of Dreams* came at a time when I was at my lowest, the death of my son Dante. I submitted the short stories I wrote many years ago, when he was an infant. I stopped caring about everything but writing. I am retired now and still trying to figure things out, hopefully writing will continue to bring me some form of peace. I hope you enjoy *Vengeance Is Mine*. I have several new projects in the works including a modern version of my first short story,

The Gunner, about a third generation psychopath that terrorizes his neighborhood until a young man, new to the area, is forced to stand up to him. I also have a story entitled, *Damien*, in the works. It is the story of a military trained assassin that works for the government. He is contracted to eliminate high profile criminals such as drug lords, human traffickers, leaders of third world countries and even serial killers that have evaded the law long enough. Thank you for reading *Vengeance Is Mine*.

www.ingramcontent.com/pod-product-compliance
Lightning Source LLC
Chambersburg PA
CBHW051129160726
47997CB00018B/873